BONES BOOK ONE

Castle Magic

by Jim Rudnick

This is purely a work of fiction. Names, characters, places and incidents are the product of the author's imagination or are used fictitiously.

Any resemblance to actual persons, living or dead, is purely coincidental.

This book may not be re-sold or given away without permission in writing from the author.

 No part of this book may be reproduced, copied, or distributed in any form or by any electronic or mechanical means past, present or future.

ISBN-13: 978-1-988144-20-7
Copyright © 2016
Jim Rudnick

For my Susan...

Bones Book Two: Castle Magic...

"Being fodder for the Spearmen was one thing, but as Javor was to learn, that meant much more than being able to dodge their spears. And his escape from the Arena meant more than saving his own life—it could mean saving his whole team and that was something he very much wanted as he dodged and ran the volley of spears.

But more than the end of the Forest Empire, was the realization that he and his team would soon be involved with the one city state on Bones, that was magical—at least that's what the story was. Castle Magic was led by humans who supposedly had magical gifts, who could not be injured or hurt and could disappear at will. Surely, there was a way to defeat these magicians, but as Javor was to learn the truth was not always a part of the story.

Join him and his team as they fight their way across Bones and see what adventures lie ahead—zombies and tribes, magicians and disciples...the list of enemies grows daily on Bones as the Boathi arrive too..."

A Message to you from the Author...

I just wanted to say thanks so so much for reading Book 3 of the Bones Series...

As my Amazon bio says, being a youngster in the 1950's meant that I was a voracious reader in what has been called the Golden Age of Science Fiction. That meant that for me, my heroes were not on the hockey rink or gridiron - but instead in my local Library where at 12 I had a full Adult card (thanks Dad!) and took out more than 5 books a week.

Everyone from Heinlein, Norton, Leiber, Pohl, Anderson, Simak, Asimov, Brackett, Gunn, Van Vogt and more....I fell in love with and eventually owned Ace Doubles of my own.

And while I never knew who wrote the Tom Corbett - Space Cadet series, I fell in love with them and they had a place of honor on my own bookcase too!

With that kind of an introduction to Science Fiction, it's no wonder that when I got my writing work done, I turned my own fictional side of my brain to writing same. It's one thing I know how to write - and a totally different matter to release same to the world - something that I've just started to work on....

Suffice it to say my own works are rooted in that Golden Age and it's that era that I'd like to one day be known as a teensy contributor to in some small way...

So once again, thanks for beginning my Bones series and wait'll you learn about the world that our hero lands on...

Enjoy and remember, in a series, characters develop and mature not the way we sometimes want...instead, it's like they have a life of their own!

CHAPTER ONE

Javor went up, higher and higher, his right leg fully extended below him. He did have a thought about whether he should take a pre-flop body position, arcing up as he spun to his left to go up and over headfirst, but he knew he couldn't do that in this case.

Instead, he just went up, and as the edge of the stage came toward him, he flexed his left wrist to spin the spear from behind his left arm, and he rolled to his right when he knew he'd cleared the stage.

As he landed, he forced the spear toward the prime disciple, who horrified by the slave who now faced him, froze in his tracks. He was starting to back up, but now he just stood on the arena stage, frozen like a deer in the headlights.

Javor landed flat on his rear end and spun quickly to kneel in front of the prime disciple in front of him, only an arm's length away.

He snarled at the prime disciple. "Tell the shieldsmen—all of them—to stand down or slaves will not be the only ones who die in the arena today."

With the spear tip only inches away from his chest, the prime disciple yelled out at the top of his voice, "Stand down! All Shieldsmen—stand down!"

"Smart ... now call over to the slave watchers, and have them release my fellow ambassadors and friends. DO IT NOW ... and live!" Javor yelled as he rose up on one knee and moved over to his left to be on the prime disciple's right side. From here, he could look down the stage and over and through the slave fencing as the prime disciple called out to the captors there to bring these slaves to the stage.

"And call down to the dog handlers—I want Khuno delivered to the stage now," he added.

At the far end of the arena, a dog handler was going into one of the dog cages calling out the dog's name. Javor waited. The prime disciple looked first one way and then the other, but he did not make a move at all with his hands or feet. He stood frozen but alive.

Minutes later, the arena now a hushed and quiet

place, Javor looked over his shoulder toward the
arena and the three shieldsmen who still stood with
spears in hand but at their sides. He looked at the
two slaves scheduled to run next and smiled once
again at the prime disciple.

"Get those last two slaves up here too—and
empty the stage of all the rest of your aides too," he
said.

The prime disciple yelled out the directions, and
a shieldsman without a spear, Javor noted, pushed
the two slaves back out of the arena to come to the
side entrance to the stage behind them. All of the
prime disciple's aides disappeared off the stage, and
now there were only the two of them. In less than a
minute, Sue and the rest of his group showed up
from the other side of the stage with Toby at the
end of the group. Bounding past them, Bixby
scampered up to lick his ankles. The two slaves
from the other side of the stage came up and all
were assembled.

Sue made sure to never get too close to the prime
disciple—but she got as close to being in his face as
she could, the spear tip just to her left as she leaned
close to the man.

She stuck a hand down into her slave tunic, and
from between her breasts, she gently pulled out a
small cylinder-shaped object and held it up for the
prime disciple to see up close. He peered at it and

then jerked back.

"I see that you know your devices like the Regime does. It's a nuke—tactical, so the crater if I set it off right here would take out everything you see within a half to three-quarters of a mile. You. Every single Empire citizen and all the buildings—including the half-built pyramid you see behind you. All I need to do is to arm the nuke, and in fifteen minutes, this is all gone," she said quietly.

The prime disciple's body began to shake as he took in Sue's words.

"We are leaving the Empire. Toby, get you and your boys up to number one," she said as she pointed right over their heads.

At the back of the stage sat a set of steps up to a platform and then a ladder up to the floater that was moored there. Toby nodded, and he and two of his ex-crewmen trotted across the stage and around the corner of the big backdrop to the steps.

"Take Bixby too," Javor yelled, and the dog followed them as he'd been ordered.

They waited, and above their heads, the floater suddenly roared into life and spun to its left to face downwind.

Sue nodded and said to the prime disciple, "You're next, follow along."

Wayne led the way and the rest of the group followed him. In one minute, the stage went from crowded to empty except for Sue and Javor.

Javor stood and looked down at the crowds who still sat silently, frozen as their leader was in jeopardy. He wanted to spear those two surviving shieldsmen who'd killed so many slaves already, but that couldn't happen. He wanted to free all the slaves, but he couldn't do that either. He put a hand on Sue's arm, nodded, and said, "Give the slaves some extra time, Sue?" and she nodded.

She held up the nuke and moved to the front of the stage. As she did, she yelled, "Slave masters—release the slaves en masse and do it now."

They began to comply, but then an argument broke out among them. The prime disciple was not in their view, and Javor wondered if they thought that meant maybe they no longer had to submit.

Sue must have had the same idea, and she spoke to the thousands there. "This is a nuke—it will kill everyone here and blow up everything you see. You will all die—or you will comply and live," she said, "and the prime disciple will be released back to you when we leave the city."

The crowds muttered and there were some dissenting arguments too, but they sat waiting.

Sue grabbed Javor and yanked him toward the backdrop to get up the stairs and ladder and onto the floater. As he turned, he stopped and pivoted, and with only two steps, he threw the spear back into the arena.

It hurtled so quickly that no one could even move —and it hit the sand directly in front of one of the shieldsmen, between his legs, and buried into the sand.

Javor could have killed the man, but he did not. He wondered why he'd spared the man.

Sue noted that and then went back to stand at the front of the stage once more. "Run … you have thirty minutes to get at least a few miles away …" she said.

The die is cast, Javor thought as he grabbed Sue's shoulder, and they both hustled behind the backdrop to mount the stairs.

Around them, they could see a large number of the previously seated guests fighting their way down the bleacher steps to get free of the arena. The slaves were now gone and had a good lead. As they got to the final ladder, Sue went up first after tucking the nuke back into her slave tunic, and Javor brought up the rear.

Where the ladder entered the lowest compartment of the floater, Wayne and Bruce quickly grabbed them, and then the ladder was kicked out.

Bruce yelled up to Toby, who was up a level and at the front of the floater. "We got 'em, Toby … go for it!"

The mooring cable was set free, and the floater
instantly began to nose up in the wind. As she rose,
Bruce led the way down the narrow corridor on the
bottom level to a major set of stairs that seemed to
go up forever. As the front stairway, it linked all the
various levels and interior floors within the floater.
Everything inside was the same shade of dull gray.

They went to their left at the first level. The aisles
were all narrow. If you wanted to get by someone,
you'd end up friends for sure, Javor thought. At the
end of this aisle, there was a large anteroom with
seats and windows for passengers to use and a
solid-looking door to the cockpit area. With a gun
trained on him, the prime disciple, who looked
more than upset, sat in the seating area. Glaring at
him, Bixby wagged a tail as Javor came over and
scratched his ears. He'd missed his dog.

"You watch him, Bix ol' buddy," Javor said, and
he grinned at the cult leader.

"You killed, what, a dozen or so slaves today. If I
had my way, I'd just take this floater up a mile and
kick you out," he said, his voice flat and nasty.

The man just sat there and said nothing.

Sue walked up to him, and fishing the nuke out
of her tunic, she pushed it in his face as he reared
back. "We gave them some minutes to run. I'm
going to arm this and set it for twenty minutes, and
then we're hightailing it outta here. The Forest

Empire dies today, Mr. Prime Nothing," she spat.

Javor banged on the cockpit door, and one of Toby's men—Andy he thought his name was—answered and let Javor inside. He walked the few steps toward Toby who was flying the floater in the pilot's seat.

Sue looked at the rows of gauges, dials, levers, and toggle switches that seemed to be everywhere in the cockpit. With only three seats in total, the space was small, and she stood to one side behind Andy who'd slid into the co-pilot's seat on the right side of the cockpit.

"Toby, if I were to set the nuke with, say, a twenty-minute delay, could we get clear before the nuke goes off?" she asked.

He tilted his head to one side and then said, "Maybe—but a full thirty minutes would be a certainty. Can you do that?" he asked.

She nodded and said, "Take us right over the pyramid, say, about fifty feet above the top.

Toby nodded. "Roger, can do."

Minutes later, the floater wheeled to its starboard side to face the wind. It sank slowly to now sit at approximately fifty feet above the topmost level area of the pyramid. Sue and Andy had already worked their way down to the lowest boarding level. Sue twisted the dial on the nuke, set the timer, and placed it in two towels. She tied a third towel and around the whole mass.

As she waited, Toby voiced their position as being optimum over the loudspeaker that had a spot just above the sliding window where Sue sat. She grinned at Andy, and the towel and its payload went out the window.

Toby had a camera pointed below the floater, and they all saw the beige towel falling, one end fluttering as it fell down. The towel-wrapped nuke lodged against a small group of free casing stones near the middle of the top level of the pyramid under construction.

Sue grinned and she and Andy went back up the stairs to sit with the prime disciple as the floater suddenly accelerated going downwind at great speed. Javor wondered what the speed of the floater might be, and as their craft went faster and faster, it climbed higher and higher too.

Sue elbowed him and said, "The blast is minimized, but we gotta be as high as possible to escape the blast as much as possible. But our pyramid is toast. Just hope the slaves got a good head start, but I'd think that as they're all running, no one's paying any attention to who's who …"

It took almost the full thirty minutes, and in the distance far behind them, a searing blast of ultra-white light appeared. The light always came first, Javor knew.

The huge sound of the detonation of the nuke followed the light. The sound was deafening—any talk of the blast being made less in this kind of a tactical nuke was horse-hockey, Javor thought.

Lastly, and as the floater bucked and rocked and was twisted to port by almost thirty degrees, came the blast radius itself. Somewhere on the floater, there was the sound of falling equipment and dishes clattering to the floor, breaking into shards and pieces. Clean up will be later … Javor thought.

Javor smiled at the prime disciple. "End of the Empire, and of your slave society too, I'd be willing to bet," he said.

The only response from the prime disciple was pursed lips and a white face.

Sue sneered. "These tactical nukes have zero rads —no radiation. They just wipe out what is within the blast radius, so you're going back to the city, Mr. Prime Nothing …

"You will have to try to remember that an ambassador is a person who commands respect—at least so that they do not get made into slaves. Ever. Remember that, it might help you in the future. I doubt it, but then who knows? Maybe your citizens will think you've done a poor job as the pyramid is gone. I wonder what your future might be like …" she said as she grinned at him broadly.

The prime disciple sat and his face paled even

more. He didn't utter a single word.

In another hour, Toby had returned the distance back to the city, and what lay below was stunningly destroyed.

The pyramid—all the way down to the footings—was gone. In the pyramid's place was a crater a few hundred feet wide. The crater had a few small fires still burning. The logs, rollers, and tracks the stones had been dragged on were all gone, but the logs burned in piles among the jumbled rock shards and chunks.

Outward from where the pyramid used to tower over the city and the arena, the crater stretched out another few hundred yards. The arena itself was gone; the sand floor once covered with blood and dead slaves was now a part of the deep crater.

The bleacher areas formed part of the rubble hiding the bloody sand from sight. Draped on part of the crater that was now the arena were black skins of what had once been floaters, all destroyed by the nuke.

Javor noted that the holding pens where he had been held were also gone as were the dog pens too, and for that he felt a twinge of guilt. He'd forgotten about them and hoped that somehow and in some way they too had gotten free.

Back toward the town itself, the nuke had taken out the first few dozen buildings in their entirety.

From what they could see, there were no bodies lying on the streets or in the crater itself, but that was to be expected as they'd all had notice about the upcoming blast.

The floater touched down right on the edge of the forest to the north of the crater, and Andy came out of the cockpit, a revolver in his hand.

"Time to leave us, Prime Disciple. On your feet," he said, and Bruce and Wayne backed him up.

Together the three of them led the prime disciple down the stairs. At the now open doorway to the world, a drop down set of stairs was already resting on the grassy ground five feet below.

Sue had followed them and nodded as the prime disciple was pushed down the stairs. He missed a step and fell out onto the ground. Javor stood by the speaker, and he hit the red button and said, "Toby, our package is off the floater. Take her up, please."

The drop down set of stairs moved up to close as the prime disciple stood and shook his fist at the floater that slowly rose and moved up to take a southeast course toward Arlington.

Javor sat in the co-pilot's seat and said, "Sorry, say that again?"

Toby nodded. "There is a lag, that can't be

counted on all the time, for all control maneuvers — pitch, yaw, and roll all work, but in their own time. You must also know the wind direction as well as where your own heading is in relation to that, and that too has something to do with response time. Best bet? Plan ahead, make your move … and then wait. You seem interested, Javor, why?" he finished off.

Javor nodded and told him of his past. The fact that he'd only been on Bones for less than a year caught Toby by surprise, but that the Boathi were aware most likely of where he and the Drake were was even more surprising.

Toby smiled at him and then tilted his head. "So … if I understand what you used to do—it was to explore planets that the Boathi had bombed and virused to see how they were, what, almost nine years later? And what did you find? How are we — stacked up against the Boathi, I mean?"

Javor toyed with the arm of the co-pilot's chair, pulling it up a bit and then down. He nodded but then held out a hand as if he was stopping Toby. "Well, I'm not the one who really knows how the comparison between us and the Boathi would be measured. I know that the few planets that we did visit, things were coming back. Some had full power and were aiming at getting back into space in less than a decade. Others were hit harder maybe, and they were a total mess still. Zombies had taken over on one planet—the marines on board the Drake said that would end when there was only one left to eat himself …"

Javor shook his head. "I do know that the Human Empire had about four hundred worlds; the Boathi more than a thousand and had superior technology too. Yet we are coming back—not yet prospering—but we are coming back, and we found just such evidence. We sent it back to HQ, of course, and would have still been on-mission if not for that damn asteroid," he said but then he shrugged too.

"Course, the accident on same got me put into the robo-doc—which did save my life when the Boathi shrapnel bombed the Drake. All the rest of the crew was killed," he said, and his voice faltered for a moment. He frowned and looked out the front viewport and down on the boreal forest well below. He took a minute or so to get back to his story.

"And, from what we know about the Boathi, they are still searching for us—the Drake, I mean," Javor said. "So anything I can learn here on Bones that might one day help me—in any way at all—to defeat the Boathi would be a good thing."

Javor pointed at the gauges on the dash. "And are these similar to, say, airplane gauges or flyers or?"

Toby nodded and starting from the far left side, he went through them all. "Your set is same as my own—the pilot and co-pilot stations have identical gauges. This one," he said pointing at the one on his left side, "is the airspeed indicator, then the attitude indicator, then the altimeter, then the heading indicator, then the vertical speed indicator, and finally the turn coordinator. Same as your side.".

Toby pointed to the space between the two stations. He listed off the larger but still important items. "Shared gauges, these ones. We've got the radio here, for both flight director systems, and local as well as VOR and NDB range and beacons too. All can be seen by both the pilot and co-pilot too which is why they're in the middle as is the normal shortwave band console too. Below all of them, is the autopilot helm with the magnetic compass there too. It's all pretty workable, and after a few hundred hours in the seat, you learn quickly where to look for the info you need instantly."

Toby smiled. "Stick is just like on an airplane— you have some experience, you said, so the controls are the same. Feet rest on the rudder controls like an airplane—but we do not have brakes on the pedals unlike airplanes. Throttles are here, between the two stations—yeah, those four levers control the air scoops and turbo-prop engines too. If you can fly an airplane, you can fly a floater too," he said, and he patted Javor's forearm as it sat between them on the arm of the co-pilot's chair.

Javor said, "No time better than right now—that okay with you?"

Toby said, "You've got the comm, Javor.

We're at"—Javor looked down at the altitude gauge in front of him—"at about twenty-nine hundred feet, moving southeast—umm … that's our heading. Course, with wind factored in is slightly more east-southeast, but I know that and will correct after, say, fifty miles. We've got, say, another two hundred miles to get to Arlington, and our speed currently is sixty-five miles an hour. We'll be there, mid-afternoon."

Javor received a confirming nod from Toby.

Putting his feet on the rudders, Javor took the stick into his hand and tried a few slow turns to right and left, keeping an eye on the gauges and noting the floater did react but slowly.

He nodded to himself and said, "Check" a couple of times as he began to get some experience as the pilot of the craft, and he grinned over at Toby after about an hour.

"Seems pretty straightforward," he said, and Toby gave him a thumbs-up back. "One thing. I hate referring to this craft as floater—did she never have a nickname?" Javor said.

Toby laughed right out loud. "Officially, this is

floater number one in the fleet—the old OilCo fleet
that is—my ex-employer before the Forest Empire
took us over. It was the best one the company had
—well, fastest anyways with biggest lifting power.
The Empire used her just a few months back to raid
the Walkerville Army Base and steal two trucks, so
she has one hell of a cargo payload. Which is why
we used to call her Zoe—for the granddaughter of
the OilGasCo CEO. Least that's what he called her
—and it sort of stuck too. She's called Zoe … and I
don't see why we can't continue with that too!" he
grinned at Javor.

Javor nodded. "Agreed, she's Zoe … and now, on
to Arlington. So nice to be above the forest too," he
said as Zoe floated on…

When the leaders of the Regime were seated at
the table, Finn spoke first. He'd not sat back to
await what the head of them all, Vera, would open
with.

"We just killed thousands of people—this is not
what I thought the Regime was all about!" Finn
said, his voice forceful and laying blame all around
the table. He blurted his words so quickly, it caught
everyone by surprise.

Maeve nodded, but her tone was anything but
agreeing with him. "We did what any smart ruling

government would do—we sent ambassadors to talk to the Forest Empire, and we also gave them a 'big stick' to back up their arguments," she said, nodding to the whole table. "The fact that they were seized as hostages, turned into slaves to help build their damn pyramid, is the issue. In those circumstances, I'd have picked the same course of action—I'd have nuked them too," she finished off and sat back. Maeve was upset and that was plain to see.

But she was still not the head of the Regime for at least a couple more days. That job was still Vera's.

Vera sighed. "We did give them that 'big stick' to use—and I agree with Maeve, it had to be used. At least they gave the population one-half hour to run away, and from the reports and the camera vids this floater recorded, few did actually perish in the nuke attack. One thing too is that they returned the Forest Empire prime disciple to the population too … why, I've no idea, but I trust that our Sue knew best," she said as she half-turned to her right to look at Finn.

"Finn, call them in, would you please?" Vera requested, and they awaited the entry of their ambassadors and new citizens.

Sue led the way and took the only extra empty seat at the table, and ranging behind her were the rest of the cadre from Maxwell, Javor, Bruce, and

Wayne, along with the Shorecroft Patrollers, Jon, Kyle, and Randy. Beside them were the new citizens of the Regime—at least that's what Vera hoped would be true. A big man, Toby, she thought was his name, stood there along with a girl and two men.

She nodded to them all, and in a surprise move, she rose at her place and clapped her hands together. Finn was on his feet in seconds to also applaud, and eventually the table full of Regime leaders was all clapping loudly.

Sue was blushing. Javor and Jon were sheepishly looking down at their feet in embarrassment, and even the new ones, were all looking somewhat flustered.

Vera sat back down and requested that Sue share the details of the mission.

Sue began the whole story of their mission, noting that they had lost a Shorecroft Patroller in the river and the rest of the harrowing trek north to the Empire. She informed the leaders they were never accepted as true ambassadors but were jammed into slavery immediately, and as slaves, the rope had become important to each of them to avoid the whip.

She shared how Javor had saved the water girl but had accidentally killed a slave master and been sent to the slave sacrifice games and how his high jump had saved them all. That got a big and rousing cheer from the group before the leaders, and she finished her story with the way they'd applied the nuke and then dropped off the prime disciple on top the wreckage of his society.

The leaders were happy they'd escaped and said so as they grinned at the group before them.

"Sue and the rest of our ambassadors—well done!" said Vera. "We were shocked to learn what the Empire had done in enslaving you but are happy, happy that you were able to both escape as well as provide a serious blow to the Empire too. Not only is their pyramid in ruins, but I'd think that their society is also adrift too. Nothing can much help the voices of rebellion who point out that their god has forsaken them as they rise up against the disciples. We suspect that the Empire will be a falling star in the north, and we have already sent out teams to look for new citizens who might be interested in coming over to the Regime as citizens. Which leads me to you four," she said as she looked at Toby.

He was big with hands like hams and scarred knuckles that showed decades of hard manual labor. He had brownish hair that was thin on top and was heavily muscled, yet he had a sense of movement that made him seem light on his feet as he nodded to Vera and took a step closer to the table.

"Ma'am, I'm Toby, and I'm a pilot—floater pilot that is, or was maybe—for the old OilGasCo company way in the north, in the New Liskeard area. We used to use the floaters to slowly scan the mountains and the boreal forests, using deep-scan technology, to find natural gas deposits or oil deposits … P90s we used to call 'em. Means that after we scan, then set down a team for drill testing, that we know that the oil or gas reservoir is both proven and recoverable too. The P90 tag means probability is ninety percent, Ma'am," he said, and one could tell he knew his oil and gas exploration, Javor thought, as Toby went on.

"We were overrun by Empire disciples at night, and they killed about half the scientists and riggers. Those of us who were floater crews were in our own separate encampments, so we were just hustled aboard and taken back to the city to become slaves. They obviously had folks who could fly a floater as not a single one of us who used to do that were asked to fill in. We just pulled granite blocks up ramps for them—so I wanted to say right up front, Ma'am, that we are not Forest Empire citizens. We'd like that known right off the bat," he said and beside him, the girl patted him on the shoulder.

She was about eighteen, blonde, and would have

been what you'd call pretty, Javor thought, but she
always had a sad, sad face on, he knew from the
weeks when they'd shared a rope on the pyramid.
She had lived with them and had been more than
agreeable to help with Sue's wounds, cleaning the
dressings and whatnot. But at night, she hid her
head under her single blanket and cried. Her
whimpers and sobs had been so very quiet but
lasted hours.

Toby looked over at the group beside him and
held out his arm. "We would like to ask for refuge
here in the Regime. I would ask on our behalf that
we become citizens and all that this might entail —
and I speak for all of us, right?" he said, and that
got tentative smiles all around.

The blonde young woman stepped forward.
"Ma'am," she said to Vera, "could I ask a question,
please?" Her voice was small and yet forceful.

Vera nodded. "Yes, child, go ahead."

The blonde nodded back and said, "I ask this
because of who I am. I am a twin — my sister was
taken from me by a disciple as soon as we got to
Empire city, and I've not seen her since. I … being
a twin means that my life is tied to hers … and I
miss her terribly and hope that she was able to get
away from the city before the nuke. Our village is —
well, was — well north of here, and I'd ask that if any
teams are sent out to look for survivors of the

Empire, that I be allowed to go too, Ma'am. If that might be allowed, Ma'am," she said, her voice now plaintive.

Vera looked over at Maeve for a moment and then back at the girl. "Youngster, I do understand what you're going through and can promise that if you become a Regime citizen, you shall be allowed to join a team going up to look for survivors. Perhaps, you might find your twin sister, I do not know—but the effort you make you shall be allowed to make—you have my word on that," she finished off.

There was more talk on various subjects related to the mission and the tasks to be carried out by the mission team members. The leaders requested that Toby take a full inventory of the floater including all equipment and especially the tanks that held fuel and helium. Bruce and Wayne were charged with the duty to help him. Sue, Javor, and Jon were asked to return for more conversations when the meeting reconvened after a lunch break. The rest were excused and allowed to find barracks and go to the quartermaster for belongings and food too.

The captain was scratching his ear socket once more, his dewclaw almost embedded in same, and the rasp was loud all over the bridge of the *Sophon*.

The final report on this planet was due—and the AI was playing its computing chimes as it worked on the summary for them.

It had taken almost twenty-three complete days to map this planet, looking for the human ship, the Drake, and its crew.

They had taken a complete grid-based scan of every single continent. They had searched with all of their superior technology for power footprints. Be it nuclear, hydro-power, solar, wind, or tidal units—they had searched for them all. They had covered the ground for landing sites or scars as the Drake had been damaged. They had used the dark side of the planet too, fully looking at every single large conglomeration of lights indicating populations and the consumption of power.

Not a single blessed thing had been found except for one single location where nuclear power might be the focus.

They had engaged their teleportation device as well, transmitting down a few security force personnel to check on a suspicious nuclear plant that appeared to be under construction but to no avail. The small security force had appeared within the actual control center for the new plant, buried within a mountain in the far eastern continent's range of mountains. They had surprised the locals and had been able to take the plans and similar materials that showed that the plant was years away from being ready to test nuclear fission. The fact that they had to kill more than a dozen white-coated scientists meant nothing to the Boathi. They were at war, and as such, their personal force field belts prevented them from being injured at all. The humans were not armed, but some fought back, throwing equipment and even beakers at the security team, which bounced harmlessly to the floor.

Not a single security team member was injured, of course, and not a single scientist was allowed to live.

This planned nuclear plant was number one on their bombing list and would be leveled, the captain knew.

But yes, there were other signs that after the years since the bombing, the local populations were once again growing.

There were new industries springing up—but with power being at such a premium, they were few and yet continued to grow, they'd noted. That had meant a request to send down a hail of bombs to take out such new beginnings, and they'd been told to await their final report, which was due momentarily.

The captain looked over at the sub-alternate who was at the helm of the ship and stared at the reptile.

His green eyes bored into the underling as his impatience grew.

The sub-alternate knew he was being glared at and kept gently hitting the SUBMIT button on his console, almost begging the *Sophon*'s AI to answer and let them know the summary report for this planet.

But it was no avail. The ship's AI continued to chime every few seconds as the report was being generated.

The rasp of the captain's dewclaw filled the bridge with the scratching sound, and the crew waited.

There was a triple chime, and the sub-alternate announced quickly, "Captain … AI has found that there is no evidence at all of the Drake on this planet. That includes all power footprints as well as deep-ocean scans too," he said.

It was to be expected, they all knew, that the exhaustive scan of the planet turned up no trace of the Drake.

One down, the captain thought. He turned to his console and sent the report to Boathi Supreme Headquarters. On his console, the icon showing that the report had been received by the supreme commander's offices was now lit up. On the far side of the console, an icon now began to flash showing they had an incoming Ansible message for the

Sophon.

"On screen, Sub-alternate," he said, and the contents of the message appeared on the view-screen.

A map of the planet they'd spent weeks studying appeared, and more than a hundred flashing locations marked cities, towns, and small power generating plants.

"Captain, this is the list of places that we are now charged with destroying on behalf of the Boathi Empire. Should I send back a received notice and then plot out an economical and fast bombing run?" the sub-alternate at the helm inquired.

He looked at the spread of more than one hundred targets. Many were spread out pretty thinly with thousands of miles between them.

"Yes, Sub-alternate. Plot out that run. Begin here in the southern latitudes and move continent by continent—and I'd like to know when AI thinks we'd be done," he said as he now leaned forward to study the map more fully.

Some of the targets were going to be easy, and he knew their various ordnances would handle most of them easily. Some, he knew, like the tidal power stations—there were only three it seemed—were going to be tougher to destroy as they lay sometimes hundreds of yards below the waters.

"Captain, AI says it's going to take almost a

week—if we start today, that is, Captain," he said.

The captain nodded. "Begin, Sub-alternate. Notify ordnance to use our biggest and best bombs —the 4TYDs, I'd think, would be best, and make the tidal ones atomic bombs too. No sense in leaving anything or anyone alive in those areas. Oh, and tell AI I want not only bombing runs based on economy and speed, but also I want post-mortems done on each power area that we destroy. Usual items, dead, degree of destruction, loss of power to their grid estimates, and the like. And I want it soon as the bombs fall too, Sub-alternate—got it?" he asked.

The sub-alternate at the helm nodded, which once again struck him as that human trait that they'd all picked up, and he almost smiled. Not that a Boathi can really smile, he knew, but curling back the lips off his snout to show his large teeth was considered a smile nevertheless.

The captain was frustrated that Boathi Supreme had kept them out in the field now for almost a year. First had been their normal explorations of worlds that had been bombed by them almost a decade ago. Then, bumping into the Drake had sent them off on this find-and-seek of same. So far, they'd searched all the worlds the Drake could have reached with no positive results. Now, they were going back over them one by one—and he thought it was a simple case of the *Sophon* being punished for missing destroying the Drake when they'd found it in the asteroid field those many months ago. A year they'd been at this mission, and he wanted to go home—back to Boathi—and rid himself and the *Sophon* of this stupid mission.

He scratched his thigh with a claw for a moment and went on. "And once we're done here, again a full report to my console, and then we're off to— what planet is next, Sub-alternate?" he asked.

"Ceti4 is next, Captain," the sub-alternate said, his hands busy on his console as bombs began to fall beneath them.

"Ceti4 … why is that name somewhat familiar?" the captain asked, as his dewclaw rasped once more.

The sub-alternate's claws were flying on his console as he asked for history and background on the planet. He got the answers to his search, and his head bobbed from side to side as he read the data on his monitor screen.

"Captain, we made first scans of the planet Ceti4 almost ten years ago—audits said not worth the effort to colonize same, so it was scheduled for a bombing run about a year later. For some reason, that run never occurred it looks like—even though I see that the sphere ship was in place over the planet and had received the proper authorizations and such. Another ship was sent out from Boathi Headquarters, and the bombing took place albeit a bit later, but still—we wiped out ninety-nine percent of the population, ended almost every single power generating plant planet-wide, and we never found out what happened to that missing ship. At least that's what the archives say, Captain," he finished off.

"So should be an easy target now. Engage," the captain said, as once again the sub-alternate's claws flew across his keyboard, and the ship went to faster-than-light speed.

CHAPTER TWO

Maeve held onto the sleeve of Vera's shirt and shook it once more. "Vera, for God's sake, woman … you're stepping down, but I still need your expertise, your counsel, and yes, your sense of what's right when it comes to governance. While I'll be the head of the Regime next week, what I need is someone who can help—right here. Not on that floater hundreds of miles away," she said exasperatedly.

Vera nodded as she swallowed the last of the excellent cupcake that Finn had somehow once again found for their lunch and swiped her lips with her napkin. "Maeve, you're ready. You need to take the reins, and that's the way that I see it. I will be the ambassador to go to Shorecroft and meet with them—and if they're willing, add them to our own citizens as a state within the Regime. That, I believe I can do, and that, I believe is exactly how the Regime should grow. State by state and that takes some doing, but with the help of Jon and his patrollers, I think we can win them over," she answered as she looked into her successor's eyes.

In less than a week, Vera would step down as the leader of the Regime, and Maeve would take over with Nixon moving up to be her number two, and that would last the same two years as their time in those positions. That Vera was now stepping down meant that Maeve would be responsible to find a suitable replacement for her on the leader team—something that was always hard to do. Finding good citizens with a sense of responsibility to the whole Regime was one thing. But talking them into coming onto the leader team for what would be a decade-long position was the hard sell.

Vera remembered that Jason had talked her into it those many years ago. He'd visited her in person at her small shop where she sold those arts and crafts she so much enjoyed, and he'd bought some as well. She grinned now, *wondering if he had just thrown away those items once she'd agreed to sit on the leader team, but she really had no way of checking.*

Jason had taken a long roam out into the wilderness years ago and had never returned. She was saddened by that, as he had become such a good friend, and she hoped that wherever he was, he was okay.

Maeve tugged once more on her sleeve, breaking her foray into those old memories. "Vera—yes, you can certainly be the ambassador to go and get the Shorecroft city into the Regime—but after that, you must return. Do I have your word on that?" she asked.

Vera nodded but held up a hand, palm up. "Yes, but remember that I'm not the leader of the mission —that would be, well, Sue, I'd guess. What I think should happen is that we go to Shorecroft to meet with their government and try to win them over. Then we'd float over to Maxwell, to return Sue and her cadre to their proper area. Javor … well, I've not thought out what we should do with him— perhaps you have some ideas? In any event, after Maxwell, we'd come back home. Does that sound like a good set of mission goals for you?"

Maeve toyed with the empty cupcake wrapper, its contents eaten with pleasure just a few minutes ago. She twisted it round and round on her plate, and little crumbs flew off the paper. This was Maeve considering, Vera knew, and that often took a few minutes, or sometimes she didn't think before she answered.

She liked it more when the new leader would think first. But then we're all different, now aren't we? she thought.

"I think you're right. That's what the mission should try to accomplish. With radio communications now so much easier as the floater has fully compliant shortwave bands, we can stay abreast of all happenings on the mission. You will need to establish some kind of a callback pattern for us too, I'd think. Sue and her cadre … she is pretty much one of our best 'in the field' people we've got —all those years in her previous marine training, I'd think, has made her a real bonus for us. Here's an idea I've been pondering," she said as she leaned in toward Vera at their table.

"Why don't we—well, why don't I create a new field position? Sue will be our first regional cadre leader. She'll be responsible to find and train each of her own area cadre leaders, beginning with her own replacement for Maxwell. We'll need one for Walkerville too, I'd suspect, right away as well. She would be charged with the duty to protect her region, composed of as many areas as we think are needed. She will need transport so that'd be another truck taken from the Walkerville base. In fact, that's been bothering me too. Maybe it's time to take over the old military base—rid the whole town of its zombies, both smart and dumb, and then Sue can appoint a new area leader for same," Maeve said, her voice still confidential here in the lunchroom, but she was making sense, Vera realized.

"Or maybe, Sue runs her own region out of the old army base—as her center of power," Vera offered up as a competing idea.

Maeve tilted her head—she's thinking once again, Vera thought.

"Bingo! Great idea—do you see why I want you here and right beside me?" Maeve said as she clutched Vera's forearm.

Vera nodded but reached over to take Maeve's hand off her arm. "Well, yes, but I could have said that in a radio conversation too, Maeve. But I think that this is a great way to go—for the Regime and its brand new leader." She grinned as she wet a forefinger, dabbed up some of the cupcake crumbs on her plate, and stuck that finger into her mouth.

Maeve grinned back. "Done. So, Ambassador, what will you need to do to get the Shorecroft leaders to join us?"

As Vera began to list what she thought she might need and what she might need to promise, Finn approached them but stood off to one side until she finished her list.

"Vera, the meeting time is about now ..." he said.

She nodded at him, and as she and Maeve got up to go back down the hall here in the Arlington Armory to the meeting room, she smiled at him as they all made for the door.

#####

It was not good news, but then again, as Toby said once again, it wasn't all bad either.

"Helium is low. We're still good, and we'd have, say, at least a thousand hours of lift—but if we can, we should find more helium as soon as possible. Nothing worse than a floater that can't float," he said, and his grin was odd, Javor thought.

"Helium. Sorry, none in my pack, but you know I'm going to ask—where on Bones do we get helium? Don't think that Arlington has many 'Helium-R-Us' type shops," Javor said, and that got a real grin from Toby.

He nodded too and patted the tank they were kneeling in front of up in the rafters of Zoe, their floater.

"Helium was a byproduct that we found—well OilGasCo found, I mean—in many locations on Bones. All in the north. All our own discoveries were near New Liskeard, our home base—well, within, say, five hundred miles of same. We do know that other oil exploration firms found more too, further west near Patch Bridge, I think, and much more northerly too near Moss Hall too. But those I know little about—we need helium, and we'll need it within, say, a thousand hours of today."

He unhooked the tablet he'd been using to test the capacity of the four helium tanks that were fixed up in the very top of the rigid floater interior. Each was more than a hundred feet in length and had a round diameter of more than fifteen feet as well. Each had a full set of gauges and read-outs built in, and each was about the same. They'd tested all four as a part of what Toby called normal pilot pre-flight checks, and each had said the same thing.

Zoe needed some helium.

"A thousand hours," Javor said, figuring as he did so. "So how many hours from here to Shorecroft and back?" he asked.

Toby cocked his head and looked up as he did the math. "Well, at, say, normal cruising speed of eighty miles an hour, it's like three or four hours there. Then back, so less than ten hours," he said.

"Sounds like it'd be well within this thousand-hour limit, yes?" Javor queried.

Toby shook his head but did hold up a hand in a cautionary way. "Yes, but if there's one thing I know—it's that there's always issues with floaters. Zoe may have lots of float time left, but every single second she's afloat comes off that thousand hours. A gentle reminder that we need helium, Javor," he said, and he clapped him on the shoulder as he stood up and stretched.

Within the rigid floater, catwalks were built into

the aluminum beams, and sills, purlins, and trusses had all been made with the support of the craft as the number one item of concern. But, knowing that maintenance and support were also important, the people who had built Zoe had also built in ways to access the various items within the rigid shell via catwalks.

Toby led the way, and Javor followed him carefully along the long catwalk to the ladders that went down in the center of the floater. They took their time, and in about ten minutes, they were back on the second floor of the floater, near the large dining room. They entered same, and Rick, the Shorecroft Patroller, nodded to them and took two more trays out of the large fridge off to one side. He popped them into the quick oven, and in moments, they were enjoying their lunch.

"Tastes sort of like dog," Toby said as Bixby wandered over to sit and look at Javor.

"Never tasted dog," Javor said as he fished through what looked like gumbo and found a chunk of fish. He forked it up and then laid it down on the floor beside him.

Bixby stared at the food, then at Javor, and then at the food as if he were watching a tennis match.

"Okay, Bix … eat it up, son," Javor said, and no sooner than he finished talking, Bixby was licking his lips, the chunk of fish long gone.

"Did feed him this morning," Rick said from the far side of the room, "but that dog is always hungry."

"So, Shorecroft—we take the new ambassador there, she convinces them to join us, and we come back. There's going to be us, Sue and the boys from Maxwell, and Jon and the patrollers. Jessica is on this one too, and I think that Vera has a couple of aides as well. Say there'd be like a dozen of us in total with liftoff scheduled for three days from now," Javor said.

Toby nodded. "Number of passengers is nominal and won't affect our float time," he said.

"So, Shorecroft, then home … say it takes a week, how many hours is that?" Javor said.

"One hundred and sixty-eight—off of our thousand. Leaves us like eight hundred and thirty-two hours or about another month of real time," Toby said as he dug into his gumbo with delight.

Javor nodded and asked, "how far is it from Shorecroft to New Liskeard?"

Toby smiled. "Already did that math. It's like six hundred miles, or at our cruising speed, about eight hours away."

"And as I understand it, Zoe doesn't care if the hours are spent holding over one spot, like being moored right here in Arlington or on the way at full cruising speed, right? Matters not to her?" Javor questioned.

Toby nodded as he chewed and swallowed his food before answering. "Matters not a whit. Float time is float time—fuel we spend on the engines for thrust. Gas we have lots of ... it's helium that we need," he said.

Javor nodded and then a thought occurred to him. "If we, say, go to New Liskeard right after Shorecroft and find helium, what's to prevent us from not only filling up—but taking, say, an extra tank or two along so we can lengthen our float time. Zoe will carry same, right?"

Toby stopped in mid-chew. "Um ..." he said as he was sliding the mouthful to one cheek. "Yeah, that'd work. Helium tanks weigh like nothing, but we'd need to find them and install them STAT, I'd think. When full, Zoe can last almost ten thousand hours of float time—and with an extra set of tanks at fifty percent capacity, that'd give us some real breathing room, float time-wise."

Javor nodded. Vera. Gotta go see Vera to get some tanks and then to okay the New Liskeard extra flight time. He smiled at Toby. "Good. Let me see what I can do."

High above the ground, Zoe floated and made good time at first. The floater's heading was south by southwest, toward Shorecroft from Arlington, and at the cruising speed of almost seventy-five miles an hour, it did look like an easy trip.

Twice, they'd dropped down over the Badlands as they were called to look at what seemed to be recently torched villages, the smoke still pouring up from same. Toby had asked Vera, who was in charge of the whole mission on the floater, if it was okay that they drop down—but not enough to put them in any jeopardy—and she'd agreed with the proviso to keep them safe.

Over the first village, just a scant hour south of Arlington, the smoke was fading as the fires were at least a day old. The village had been one, Sue said, that had been a strong one with more than a hundred residents, she thought. Vera agreed and then added that whoever had set fire to the village would have had to be slavers.

"Not many others will invest the time and effort and risks to ravage a simple village," she said.

And Javor nodded at that. *In his experience, anyone who would invade a village to kill and to take slaves as well as fresh food and ravage looking for arms and treasure would be stupid to leave anyone alive behind them.*

"Lindos is where they're bound," Sue said, and that got stares all around as the free city of Lindos was known to be a city where anything and everything was both allowed and revered.

"We've been in the air, what, half an hour, and already we see slaver workings," Bruce said from the rear of the seating area off the cockpit.

"Seems to me that the smoke ahead means that, yup, these slavers are raiding every single village between Arlington and Lindos and taking their spoils to Lindos. I'd bet on it," Jon said as he shook his head.

Vera motioned to Toby up front in the cockpit. "Toby, the village ahead? Take us down a bit so we can see what's happening, but be ready to zoom up if there's any current action."

He nodded and Zoe began to drop slightly as the miles passed and the plume of thick black smoke got closer.

As Toby looked at the gauges in front of him, he turned his head to the rear to speak to Vera. "Ma'am, the village is, like, fourteen miles from the one behind us—on the shores of that small lake— can you see it?" he asked as Zoe floated ever closer.

They all could see it. There were many small fires still raging as village huts burned. From the thousand feet or so up in the air that Zoe was floating at, they could still see figures lying on the ground, still and not moving. Over at the edge of the village, where the forests started back up, there was a line of what appeared to be slaves. The slaves were in neat little lines, two by two, and all craned their heads to look up at the floater. There were slavers looking up as well, and a few shot arrows up at them, but they never came close.

"No gunfire," Toby reported, and Bruce nodded as he scanned the groups of people below.

"Wish we could help those slaves," Javor said pointedly.

"We can't at this point," Vera answered him and held up a hand to stop his protestations that were about to follow. "We can if we get to Shorecroft and form an alliance that will include the lands between Arlington and them. Lindos, however, appears to be another matter," she said.

Below them, the line of more than fifty slaves was being herded out of the cleared lands of the village and into the forested edge beside when Jessica half-screamed, "Wait!"

She was at the window on the starboard side of the floater, directly behind the cockpit, and she was pointing down at the lineup of slaves now only six hundred feet below. Her arm was trembling as she pointed.

"See the lineup of slaves at the end? See the young blonde girl at the very end of the left-hand chains? That's Jennifer! I know that's my sister! Look at her ... go down Toby, we must save her." She was screaming now.

Vera and Javor were already looking out of the starboard side windows, and they too could see a young woman, blonde as well, at the end of the lineup of slaves being herded into the trees.

"We can't go down there, Jessica," Vera said. "We are a dozen, and we saw more than twice that of the slavers alone—and there's bound to be more we can't see too," she said, trying to calm the young hysterical girl in front of her.

Javor mentally agreed with Vera; the odds were too stacked against them.

"If it is your sister, then as a slave, she's being taken to Lindos for sale at what might be quite a high price. That'd mean that the slavers below would fight long and hard to keep us away from kidnapping her back."

"But," Sue said, "we may be able to help in Lindos if Vera would okay a stop there?"

Vera sat back in the seating alongside the windows and looked at Sue. "Do you mean, if we were to stop in Lindos, we might find a way to get the girl away from the slavers?" she asked.

Sue nodded and grinned too. "We could even buy her maybe—then there'd be no worries about risk. Course, being in Lindos is always a risk—and then showing up in a floater would also be a further risk too, wouldn't it," she said, as her voice suddenly dropped.

"I can set down a small group with a walkie-talkie. You can find the girl, free her, and then we can arrange to pick you all up after that. That I know can work—except I wonder what the price might be for Jessica's sister … more perhaps than we have with us?"

They all thought on that for a minute or two.

Money on Bones did not exist anymore—but credits still did. One traded for something and got credits in return which would normally be accepted by others in exchange for other goods and services. Not always, though, and that was a problem sometimes. But the bartering of items always worked, they all knew.

Sue smiled. "Maybe we can trade some of our advanced weapons for the girl … say two combat shotguns with ammo for one girl?"

They had all visited the Arlington Armory and had taken once again arms that each of them found comfort with. Javor had his big mag combat shotgun that Bruce had insisted he try, and he was very happy with same. Vera had also ordered some extra items to be stored on Zoe that would serve as the floater's small armory too, and that was always a barter item worth investing in.

"Who knows … but we can try. Failing that, we'll simply wait 'til after the sale of Jennifer, follow the new owners, and take her. That I know we can do too," she said, and that got some shrugs, but eventually all present agreed.

Lindos would be their next stop in only an hour more.

#####

The marketplace was crowded, loud, and busy as usual, and the throngs had to watch their steps as they made their way down the crowded aisles that were jammed with hawkers of everything one might want.

On one side and ahead of the man who led the small party of similarly clothed group members, Lindos merchants tried to ply the shoppers with technology. New small radios were popular, it seemed, but the battery life was short. There were additions that one could make to a walkie-talkie that would allow it to send out a beacon that could be tracked from afar, which sounded like a good thing too.

The leader of the small group of six, a black mage, stood almost six and a half feet in height. His hair was dyed the shade of soft violet like nightshade, and his eyes were piercing and bright. The robe around him was open on both sides, yet around his waist, it was gathered by a thin silver belt with a large purple buckle in the center of his waist.

He appeared to be "in shape" as some might call it, and he walked with purpose, stopping only to listen to a hawker in a very few instances before striding on. He appeared to be on a mission, and as he and his similarly clad group reached a major intersection of aisles, he waved over one of his group to talk.

"Banshee Golin, can I ask—the location could not be pinpointed better than what we have?" he said, holding out two arms in a sweeping gesture. It was obvious that he was somewhat upset that in the big Lindos marketplace, he had not found what he was looking for.

"Mage Gelert—I am sorry, but the best we could find, data-wise, was that arms would be here mixed in with the technology vendors, Mage," he said, his voice apologetic.

It was true they were somewhat at odds with what lay all around them, but the black mage was not happy. Yet he nodded and took the first right-hand aisle that presented itself and had to walk by more than a dozen more technology hawkers pushing everything from wrist vid players to fitness bands for one's arm. He shook his head time and time again and then stopped cold.

Ahead of them on their right was a large set of tables, all with ugly bright yellow tablecloths, but what lay on top of them was what was interesting.

Arms. Rifles, carbines, shotguns, machine guns, grenade launchers, and more.

He beckoned to the rest of his group, and they all went to stand in front of the tables, but there were already customers in front of them, so he paused to listen.

"More than a dozen shots per second is what I'd call an alley cleaner," the vendor said as he held up a large fully automatic rifle of some type. It was an off-world manufactured item as the blue sticker showed on its side. That meant that should it ever need any kind of maintenance or repairs, it was not going to be a likely possibility.

"Yes," the young man in front of the Mage said, "but at that price and the needed ammo, I'd be broke before I could even buy those dozen shells." He swiped his hand at the vendor and pushed away from the table.

The mage and his group took up the front row and looked at the vendor who laid down the automatic rifle and said, "Yes, fellows, something I can sell you?"

The mage nodded and pointed at the carbines off on one side. "Carbines—how many of that model do you have?" he said in a matter-of-fact tone.

The vendor's eyes narrowed, and he pulled at his black goatee as he considered his answer before responding. "As many as you might need—Mage, right?" he asked.

The mage bowed his head slightly and nodded.

"Then I have at least twenty here today—and more I can get tomorrow should you require more than that, Mage," he said. His voice was polite and yet he was still selling. "And might I add that we don't often see visitors from Castle Magic here … so this is a pleasure." He smiled.

The mage held out his hand, and the vendor scooped up the carbine off the table and placed it gently in the mage's hands. He sighted down the barrel first, noting the blued steel, the easy to use sights, the solid wood fore stock, and butt plate end. "Oiler seems somewhat off center," he said, noting that back on the stock, the sling oiler was not up to par.

"Mage, that's because this carbine is an oval cut stock—you're used, perhaps, to the older I-cut stock, which is now deprecated, Mage," he said nicely. Correcting a customer was always a touchy item, and this being a mage made it tougher.

The mage nodded. Correct answer. This vendor knew his weapons. "I would like to purchase thirty-six of these carbines—exactly like this one. No substitutions and no fiddling with the standards either, vendor. Can you supply that many—and at what price and in how many days?" the mage asked.

The vendor took half a step back, not because he was surprised at the size of the mage's needs, but because he was suddenly going to be rich. He smiled and ran the numbers in his head as he looked at the two pallets of weapons in their original cases behind him.

"Mage, by tomorrow, I can have all thirty-six carbines—exactly like this one—here for you. For that, I will have to charge you at least seven hundred credits each—or a total of twenty-five thousand credits. Will that be a deal to your liking, Mage?" he asked.

The black mage nodded and held out his hand, and Banshee Golin once more stepped forward to join him at his side. From under his robe, he took a pouch and placed it on the table between his mage and the vendor. He opened it and counted out the twenty-five thousand credits in one-thousand-credit notes, placing them in a pile. He resealed the pouch, and it disappeared under his robe once more.

The vendor gulped, as the mage pushed the pile toward him.

"You have just been paid in full, vendor. I will return at this time tomorrow to receive our arms. Please, do not let anything affect your ability to complete our deal, you know what can happen," he said nicely, but the threat was there.

People who tried to forgo a deal made with anyone from Castle Magic learned they would pay dearly for their deceit.

But the vendor who obviously knew the same stories was too busy nodding up and down to even think such a thought.

"Tomorrow, Mage … same time, your arms will all be here. I'll have them all displayed for you to check them all and then package them all together for your group to take them away. No charge for the dolly either, Mage … my treat, Mage," he said as he gathered up the stack of credits and jammed them down into his tunic pocket.

The group from Castle Magic walked away, their business done for today, and only the pickup of the new arms tomorrow was still on their list.

They backtracked out of the aisles slowly retreating out of the huge Lindos market and back along a major thoroughfare toward the city gates. Once there, the security teams, who manned all of the access points to Lindos, nodded them through, and they walked down the road ahead dodging small wagons with produce and a group of incoming slavers too.

As they slowly climbed the near hillside, they left the road and walked on the sparse grass and weeds on the hillside until they reached the crest. Behind them, Lindos, the walled city, lay against the wide shoreline of the sea just a few hundred yards distant.

The mage went over the hilltop first and down a few yards so that he and the rest of the group would be hidden from anyone who might want to watch. He smiled at the group, said, "On my mark," and reached for the large purple belt buckle on the silver belt that circled his waist.

"Three … two … one … MARK," he said, and they all pushed one of the buttons hidden behind the belt buckle and disappeared.

All six. Gone in an instant … like magic.

CHAPTER THREE

While they were trying to find a way to land some of the group surreptitiously, Toby was still cursing at the winds.

"With this kind of tailwind, I'm having a dickens of a time trying to keep her low and still get us close enough. Sue, we gotta stay, like, at least five miles out of Lindos or we'll blow our cover," he said, his voice exasperated as he worked the stick and the rudder pedals at the same time.

Tailwinds were notorious for creating difficulties with the handling of the rigid aircraft, and Toby was certainly working hard at keeping them hidden yet high enough to not worry about the forests around Lindos.

"Let's call this place beside the brook and the row of huge pines spot number one. If we need to pick you up here, then it's spot number one, okay?" he queried Sue.

Sue nodded after getting a thumbs-up from Javor. "Good, Toby, spot number one it is," she said, and she stared out the windows to imprint the spot in her memory. Lindos was three or four miles to the east, and here, the tall original growth pines could hide Zoe from all but eyes up close.

"Then remember back when I had to come down the ridgeline, and we flew across that huge field of those yellow flowers? Let's call that spot number two. It'll be our backup for pickup, agreed?" he asked.

"But spot number two is further away and somewhat north of spot number one—is that a good idea?" Vera asked the group seated behind the cockpit.

Javor nodded but before he could say anything, Jon, the Shorecroft patroller, spoke up.

"Always good to have two pickups—course, this is standard in most mission extraction programs. We would do the same—and the second spot is usually never used—unless there's trouble at spot number one. But this looks—to me at least—pretty benign. We'd be three miles outta Lindos, through what looks like heavy forest, and I see not a single pathway coming here from the bank of trees, so we should be fine," he finished up and got nods from some too.

Javor agreed with him but knew that sometimes a mission had to split up—especially if they were carrying wounded—and having spot number two farther away might be problematic, but that was negative thinking, he rationalized and smiled.

Toby skillfully fought the tailwinds as he turned the floater slowly to face now into the wind. The team who was going into the city assembled below where the landing ramp would drop out and onto the grounds.

Javor was taking point, so he led the way down the ramp that dropped out onto the grass just beyond the brook bubbling away behind them.

Jon and Kyle, two of the Shorecroft patrollers, came next followed by Sue and Wayne who were the last of the five away team members. Each carried a backpack and had an extra weapon strung over their shoulders. Javor had two of the combat shotguns, each with forty-shell magazines, and while he'd hate to part with one of them, there was the matter of Jessica's sister, so he shrugged it off.

As Wayne stepped off the ramp, Javor threw a thumbs-up to Toby who was above them in the cockpit, and the floater slowly lifted back up as the ramp was being automatically lifted back up and into place on the belly of the floater. The engines on each side spun somewhat louder as the ship, still nose-first into the wind, lifted a few hundred feet more and made its way back north by northwest to hide in the range of low mountains that were in that direction.

Zoe would be kept about those twenty miles away, it had been agreed to, and when Sue's team was ready for pickup, they'd radio in on the walkie-talkies for which spot they'd be on. Simple and neat, Javor thought, but he'd been an explorer far too often on too many missions to ever count on the simplest of plans coming off perfectly.

He turned and walked across the brook, stooping to take a cupful of water with a hand and smiled at the team behind him. "Cold and clean—like I hope the mission goes," he said, and Wayne chuckled.

Sue tilted her head as if to say let's hope so, and she waved him on.

Javor was on point and he picked the path they would follow. He aimed at two trees ahead and slowly made his way through the broken overgrowth toward them. Once there, he looked ahead again, and all he could see were the dark boles of trees in front of them. No real path could be seen, and with the mixed species of trees, the sunlight rarely reached down to the forest floor. He walked on and after a few hundred yards, he held up his hand to stop the group spread out behind him.

And he listened. He listened hard and after a moment, he could hear small forest sounds. Bird calls—not many but a few. Something rustled under the log over to his left as it tried to hide. He looked up and saw a few birds.

If and when you find yourself in the woods, you must try to determine if you are the stranger in the midst of the woods—or not, Javor recalled from his previous experiences.

If so, like now, there was nothing to worry about.

But if not, if you found the woods dead silent even though you'd stopped to quietly rest—there was something else in the woods. Javor absently scratched the big scar on his left biceps. Something that was perhaps hunting you.

But not this time, he thought, as he waved them all on and continued to lead the way to Lindos now only a few miles ahead. He led the way carefully and yet always on guard for anything that hit his senses. Once, he thought he could smell some kind of animal dung, and his right boot proved that right in one more step. He wiped off the boot as best he could on the short undergrowth.

He was in a small glen—devoid of any trees— that was only about thirty feet across, and he moved quickly through the area and then back into the trees again.

It was getting brighter ahead of him. The canopy

of leaves overhead was ending as the forest thinned out—and Lindos lay ahead. He reached the edge of the forest and stopped at a big oak tree with acorns scattered beneath it. He peered around the tree at the lay of the lands ahead.

Over a field of what looked like cabbages from here, about two hundred yards away, was the walled city of Lindos. Dark brown adobe-type mud walls of only a dozen feet in height ran for about a half a mile in each direction. A gate that had soldiers or a security team just standing around was almost dead ahead.

As he watched, the rest of his team caught up to him and took semi-hidden positions near him to look out and get some reconnoitering done.

As they all watched, a wagon being pulled by what Javor would call a mule—yet it had six legs for some reason—was being led by a farmer who approached the gate into the city.

They were too far away to overhear anything, but after a short conversation, the gate security team moved out of the way, and the farmer and his wagon full of crops entered the city.

Sue whispered, "Seems pretty straightforward, let's give it a shot. Follow me please, team." She stepped out from the forest into the full open sunlight.

Walking on cabbages was not a lot of fun, and

they all quickly learned to get off the rows of the cabbages and to walk in the shallow muddy drainage rows between them. Their boots got muddy, but none of them tripped. "That's a good thing," Javor said to himself as he smiled. More to add to my explorer experience archive, he thought, and he checked off too walking in a cabbage field and plodded along behind Sue.

In a few minutes, the team was standing with her in front of the security team at the gate. They had paid little attention to them as they'd crossed the cabbage field but now stood between the away team and the city gate. Each was armed, yet all their weapons pointed straight up into the sky—not at the team.

One of them looked at Sue, who stood at the front of the team, and nodded. "Welcome to Lindos. I do not know you or your friends. You are aware that Lindos is a free city, yes?" he asked, his rifle still pointed up into the sky.

"We are new to Lindos, but we would like to enter to see the city and to go to your markets," Sue said. She had copied his tone and attitude exactly—polite, yet still a force to be reckoned with should the need arise. Her weapon, a carbine with a huge mag, hung off her armored vest and pointed down at the ground.

He nodded to them. "You are welcome. This is a

free city—people come to Lindos for many reasons, but one thing all who come here do is to buy and sell anything from slaves to cabbages," he said as he pointed over Sue's shoulder at the huge field they'd just crossed.

"We are Lindos security. We provide the law, and we enforce the law. Enjoy and be a good visitor and all will be well, but remember, if security finds you've cheated or stolen or hurt someone, we don't have courts and lawyers. We have these," he said as he hefted his rifle up and down in the air. "Welcome," he said, and he and his small team of five moved out of their way to let them enter the city.

Sue smiled at him and walked ahead, followed by Javor, Jon, Kyle, and Wayne.

As they passed through the gate in the wall, Javor noted that the wall was about a foot and a half thick and topped with shiny broken glass, maybe to make scaling the wall an expensive way to enter or leave the city. Inside the gate was a wide city street, leading inward, that was sparsely populated with Lindos citizens. A few women with children were outside hanging laundry over the sides of balconies.

They took no real tactical formation but simply walked ahead, inward toward the city center. As they crossed the odd side street and went through the intersections, Javor noticed that the city was a bit quieter than he'd expected. As they moved closer to the city center, more citizens were in the streets. Some adults and the children with them had their arms full of tomatoes, corn, and other vegetables. Others were carrying boxes that looked heavy.

He shrugged. *What a citizen did in their own city was to live. That was all.*

As the group got closer to what looked like a major city center, they could see a park ahead with several children playing in a green grassy area. There were benches that held mothers and even a playground too with swings, slides, and those old-fashioned merry-go-rounds that moms always yelled for their kids to stay off. As the group walked, they turned to the left side of the street and slowly went in a large circle around the park area. Ahead lay what looked like the major city markets area.

Row after row of tables with vendors barked out their wares. As he craned his neck to see as far as he could, Javor thought the aisles looked like they went on for hundreds of yards, and he grinned at just how big a market this was. Lindos was definitely a powerhouse when it came to economy, and for Bones, that was a good thing.

He walked with Wayne at his side, following Sue

who led the way, and they all stopped as she inquired from a vendor as to accommodations in the city and the location of the slaver marketplace. The man nodded, pointed back over their shoulders, and zoomed his arm down and to the left, telling them the best place to stay was the Yoli Hotel—cheap and clean and his brother was the manager—ask for Clyde, he said proudly. And slaves could be found being sold only at the slaver market—and he pointed this time ahead and down the same street they had been on.

"About halfway across town, in the eastern area, you can't miss it. Huge stage and cages and the sound of pious whimpering as they get sold," he said, laughing loudly and smiling at them.

"But would you like to trade today? I've wonderful textiles from Patch Bridge—the center of our Bones weaving areas, and they would look beautiful on you," he said to Sue as he tried to butter her up.

"That and I'd love to own one of those rifles— maybe we can make a deal," he asked, but Sue shook her head.

"Sorry, no need for cloth today—and the rifle I won't part with," she said.

He sighed and turned away to speak to a couple of women who were fingering a bolt of bright pink cloth beside him.

Sue nodded to them, pitched her head back toward the Yoli Hotel, and said, "Let's go and check in and get some cleanup time first.

"By Toby's reckoning, we're at least a day ahead of the group of slaves we're interested in. They won't show up 'til tomorrow, so let's get accustomed to Lindos first," she said as she turned back and toward the park and then off to her right toward the Yoli Hotel.

Check in. Have a shower and shave. Maybe even a nap, Javor thought.

Sounds wonderful …

#####

In the Yoli Hotel, Javor sat in the small courtyard off to one side in the center of the hotel building and drank what passed for coffee here in Lindos. It was at least hot, and with tons of milk and a bunch of those sugar cubes, it passed as coffee. "Not so much really," he said to himself as he made room for Jon to join him at the small table.

Jon looked rested and relaxed. Javor nodded and they both sipped their coffees.

Eventually, Jon put down his cup and smiled. "Great rest, nice to have been able to take the time."

Javor nodded back and the table grew as Sue came along.

"Rest are still in the showers," Sue said, and she

frowned as she tried her own coffee. "This stuff is like mud."

They slowly drank their coffees, and eventually, the rest of the team showed up. Wayne had wet hair, and Kyle was rubbing his eyes, but to Javor all looked much better after the full night's sleep.

Sue nodded. "Okay, here's what I think we should do. We will go and investigate the markets and pay particular attention to the slave area markets. If Jessica's sister appears, we will try to buy her first. If not, then we'll follow the new owners, and if needs be—then steal her away. They may not be so welcoming, but that's why we're armed. But I'm loath to lose a man—we may need to ambush them, rather than have a full firefight scenario. We okay with that," she asked, and that got grins and nods all around.

"Seems like we're going to great lengths to help out Jessica—let's not end up paying with lives," Wayne said, and all agreed with solemn faces.

Sue rose, left most of her coffee behind, and said, "Let's go then—and if anyone sees a real spot to get some real coffee, speak up!"

Once outside the Yoli Hotel, they took the side street the hotel lay on and moved toward the main Lindos street that led to the city center. More people were out today, Javor noted, and many more children too. He wondered about school and if this was a day off for the kids.

After a quick question to a mom who had two to look after, Javor caught up with the group. "Mom back there says today's a weekend day; no school or much going on, but the markets are still open, she said."

Wayne nodded and said, "No school is a good day, as I remember," and that got a laugh from most in the group.

They walked past the park and the city center areas again and approached the market side. At the main alley that stretched ahead, several shoppers and tourists filled the area

They went past a whole section where the hawkers out front of their booths offered up everything from cabbages to cloth, new tablets to old antiques, and ice cones flavored with sweets to arms like pistols and rifles too.

As they slowed down at the arms dealer section, each carefully looked for the latest releases of various weapons. *Some, like pistols,* Javor noted, *were all older used items. Rifles, however, were newer—at least some looked new and were still in cases too.*

Sue paid close attention and Javor noted the shotguns were all older than the two he carried and had much smaller magazines too.

Score one for us, he thought. He hoped that would help when it came to buying a slave.

They walked ahead toward the center of the huge market's Agora area, and eventually, they reached that spot. Sue nodded to the left, and they took a sideways path toward the left edge of the high stage that backed onto the holding pens behind the stage. Steps led up from the holding pens, which held many slaves waiting to be sold. Near the center of the stage, to their right a bit, the slave cashiers had a desk, and they were protected by a squad of Lindos security men all armed to prevent any kind of to-do. From what Javor saw, a firefight here would be a deadly exchange that would have little chance of success.

They waited. He looked over at the stag. Bare as it was, there were some posts, with chains hanging down, every ten feet or so. There were a couple of boxes too, where he thought a slave could be put up higher so the crowds could see them more easily. There was nothing else but those few things on the stage, and he thought that if that was what was needed—all that was needed—to sell human beings as slaves, it was a pretty easy business to break into.

Course, he thought, *that's if you believe in slavery itself as a business rather than as an evil entity all on its own.*

This galaxy had been cursed with that kind of thinking for thousands of generations. He'd seen slavery all across the old Human Empire, and he knew that the Boathi too had such an evil part in their history as well. At least others had told him that, and that meant that both sides of the two warring factions had the same dirty hands.

He shrugged. *Not my concern. All I need to do is to get this Jennifer out of the hands of the slavers. Buy her or ambush for her later. Should be an easy mission,* he thought and smiled.

They still waited, but there was now some action over at the cashier's desk. Three men and a woman appeared and took their seats at the table.

In front of the table was a short lineup of a few citizens and carried something to barter with, and he moved closer to listen in to those negotiations.

First up was a farmer, he thought. The man was dressed in lightweight jeans and a tank top, and he had long hair and a full beard.

"Want to know what kind of funds you'd give me for forty bushels of these," he said as he emptied out a burlap bag onto the table. Sitting on the desk now were tomatoes and zucchinis, all very ripe and ready to eat.

"Forty? Say fifty? Fifty for each? We'd offer up …" The woman looked at her peers and there were some mutterings between a few of them, and then she said, "We'd offer up a maximum of four hundred credits."

The farmer nodded and a deal was struck. Some tablet entries made, and he walked away now able to pay up to four hundred credits for a slave. Over at the far side of the stage, Javor noted, there were a few of his helpers unloading those bushels of produce, which were being accepted by the slave market personnel. By the end of the day, those vegetables would have been sold to other vendors at the markets and a profit made for the slavers.

Easy business to understand, he thought, but he knew that at its core, *the evil of people being sold into slavery was the part he couldn't get past.*

Behind the farmer came a group of women who were trying to sell handicrafts. The slave cashier refused them outright. Guess buying a quilt is not such a good deal, he thought.

Behind them was a man who offered up a collection of some jewelry—from his own family, he said—and he got more than a thousand credits for those shiny gems and gold necklaces. *Gems always work,* Javor thought. *No surprise there …*

Sue was next, and she simply placed one of their combat shotguns on the table.

"How many of these do you have?" the woman at the cashier table asked as one of the men picked up the brand new shotgun to check it out. He worked the action, took off the magazine, emptied the chamber, and fired a few blank rounds. He checked the serial number plate and the manufacturer's plate, nodded to the woman, and said, "Top quality shotgun."

"I have a few—what price do you offer for them each?" Sue answered.

The cashiers conversed and haggled quietly between themselves.

The woman turned back to face Sue. "We'd offer up four hundred and fifty credits per shotgun, if that would be acceptable?"

"Six hundred each," Sue said.

Everyone at the cashier's table sat back. After more talk and some elbowing, the woman spoke up again.

"The most we can go—our final offer—is five hundred and fifty credits each. No more," she said.

Sue nodded, picked up her gun, and returned to the group. With three shotguns, they could successfully bid as high as sixteen hundred and fifty credits for Jennifer, and that made him smile. When Javor asked the people around him, he learned slaves went for less than that, especially field slaves. The smarter and more skilled slaves who could be house slaves or used in manufacturing would bring higher prices. The highest price for a slave last year was almost two thousand credits. That slave had been a college professor.

Why anyone would have paid that much for a college professor, amazed Javor, but while he was pondering that, a slave seller walked out to the center of the stage as the sales were about to begin.

Behind him, a couple of slaves were led out to the hitching posts and shackled. The seller began to talk about the two slaves. "Twins. As twins, they're sold as a set," he announced. "These fine young men are well-trained, compliant house slaves. They have been slaves their entire lives and will obey their master no matter what."

The seller opened the bidding at one thousand credits, and the number went up slowly to almost fourteen hundred credits. He prodded, cajoled, and tried to boost the price up, but at thirteen hundred and seventy credits, those twins were sold.

The new owner sidled up to the cashier's table to sign some paperwork and take ownership of the young men. While the slaves were removed from the stage, the seller reminded the crowds they were starting today's sales with the fancies—slaves that were not meant for fields or plants but for the owners' homes.

Four more slaves were sold. A cook who was supposedly very well trained and grew her own herbs went for eight hundred credits. An older man who was a tutor for students went for almost a thousand credits. The next two slaves, a brother and sister, were sold as a set. These two were skilled at managing a master's books and accounting for their finances and went for twelve hundred credits.

Lastly, a gorgeous young blonde woman was chained to the post. "Young woman of almost eighteen years—new slave so there is no guarantee on her compliance, folks. She is a virgin, she has been schooled as well, and she is full of fire—so beware. Oh, did I mention that she is pretty?" he added.

The bidding was opened with Sue offering one thousand credits for Jessica's sister before the slave auctioneer could even name a starting price.

The young woman looked at Sue and sneered, as if she was letting Sue know she'd be an awful slave, Javor thought.

"Eleven hundred," said someone from behind them.

"Twelve," Sue said immediately.

"Fourteen," said the same voice.

"Fifteen," Sue said, her voice loud and brash.

"Sixteen hundred," that same voice said, and the seller stood there grinning as the bidding war continued.

"Seventeen hundred" Sue replied, and Javor realized she'd just added his shotgun to the pile making it four guns for twenty-two hundred credits in total. He'd be unarmed until he got back on Zoe, but that was okay.

"Two thousand," said that insistent voice from

CastleMagic

behind them.

Sue was silent.

The seller looked elsewhere in the crowd for more bidders. "Come, come buyers, we're at two thousand credits—surely there is more here who'd love this girl as a house slave?" He looked from one side of the crowd to the other, and not a single voice chimed out.

"Twenty-two hundred credits," Sue said, offering the total they could afford.

"Twenty-five hundred," said that same voice in an instant.

The seller was beside himself with joy. That was a yearly record, and he smiled as he stamped his foot on the stage. "Sold, to the mage from Castle Magic," he said.

As the team turned to watch, a man wearing a black robe, wide open on the sides yet tucked into a silver belt at his waist, stepped forward. His hair was dyed a light purple and he was very tall.

He didn't look at Sue or the team. He went straight to the cashier's table, pulled out a pouch from inside his robe, and laid it on the table.

"Take the twenty-five hundred credits," he said to the woman, who tentatively opened the pouch and slowly counted out twenty-five one-hundred-credit notes. She placed them in a pile in front of her, slowly tucked the remaining large sheaf of credit notes back into the pouch, and slid it toward the man who stood in front of her.

He signed some paperwork, Javor noted, and then two more similarly clad men came around the far corner of the stage with Jessica's sister, Jennifer, chained between them. He nodded to the cashier's table, and they all turned to leave the slave area, moving with a degree of relative haste.

Sue looked at her team and said, "Let's go— slowly and let them get a few hundred yards ahead once we're outside the city.

They followed as unobtrusively as they could, but as the city streets were sparsely populated with the big slave sale going on, they had to fall back a considerable distance to not be seen. As they approached the city gate, Jessica and her three new owners were halfway across the cabbage field. They slipped every so often on a head of cabbage.

Javor fanned out to the left with Sue in the middle and Jon on the far right-hand flank. Wayne and Kyle followed closely behind. When they reached the end of the cabbage field, they stepped into the woods and saw Jessica with the mage and his men ahead of them as they walked along the heavily forested stand of trees. With no path, they just went around tree bole after tree bole as they walked.

As they reached that little cleared glen area

ahead, they gathered into a small circle around the blonde girl, and Javor thought immediately that she was in trouble. He picked up his pace, his boots crunching on the acorns under the large oak trees.

One of the men with the mage turned in Javor's direction, and Javor halted behind an oak tree. When he peered around the oak tree, their quarry was gone, and the glen was empty.

He broke out into a lope and was quickly joined by his team. They moved through the wood stand and into the small glen. The glen was only thirty feet across, but their quarry could not be seen.

Where had they gone? They couldn't have made it through the glen that quickly.

They stopped and listened to the sounds around them.

Not a single step, a swishing branch, or the crunch of leaves was heard.

Nothing.

There was no one there.

Sue looked exasperated and she turned around to check behind her. "Where the hell did they go now?" she asked.

"If we'd a taken Bixby, maybe he could have found their scent," Wayne said.

Wherever the new slave owners had gone with Jennifer, they'd missed it, so far at least.

"Fan out, all points of the compass. Go out at a

run at least, say, half a mile and fire if you find them," she said.

Javor nodded and he took off to his left, crashing through the underbrush and around pines, hoping that if he didn't find them, he'd hear a gunshot that would signify one of his team had.

Almost a full hour later, he was back at that glen with no luck.

Sue sighed and her voice was flat. "We lost them —or they just disappeared. I am not going to enjoy telling Jessica about this, but let's get our asses back to spot number one. Wayne, let Toby know we're about a mile away or so …" she said.

Javor now plodded along at the rear of the team as they made their way. All he could about was how someone could just plain disappear out of the woods with no technology to help.

#####

His face solemn, Warlock Gonnert looked over at the group before him.

Too bad, he thought, *that I can't just wave my hand and all my problems would all disappear.*

He was more than upset, but like all rulers in society, he knew he couldn't really show his true feelings. He nodded instead and said, "Tell me more then, Banshee, about what you found."

In front of him, standing, of course, as only the

warlock sat in the temple, Banshee Gillead shifted on his feet. Gonnert could tell he was uncomfortable in relaying his mission debriefing, but it was a part of his job.

"Warlock, as ordered, we went all the way to the far side of the desert to the west of the castle. We made pretty good time, and we visited with many of the various tribes of nomads that we found. All of them were offered to join us here as full members and eventual citizens of the castle, — and some did indicate that, yes, they'd consider same. Others spurned our offers, and in one case, we were ushered out of their camp and forced to move on. We have marked the map," he said as he tendered same by putting a rolled-up document on the table in front of him, "with the locations of these groups, and we have no doubts that they will continue to stay in those places at least until the autumn rains," he said.

He knew that he was supposed to have found new citizens, and he knew that his job as one of the leaders of this mission meant that he was to be successful. Yet he had failed; he knew that too.

Warlock Gonnert nodded again, and his thoughts went to the current list of his competent staffers.

Banshee Gillead was on his list as such. Yet he'd just failed to find new converts for the castle.

"Banshee, I want to know one thing more—if I

were to send you back out on the exact same mission—even, say, by transport to make it so much easier—could you bring them in? All of them, Banshee?"

He knew asking for all of the various tribes and villagers would be almost impossible, but he wasn't really looking for results—he was looking for the passion in his banshee.

Banshee Gillead bowed deeply, rose, and said, "Absolutely, Warlock Gonnert—transport us and I will succeed this time." His voice was strong and committed.

Gonnert looked over at his aide, Black Mage Gelert, and nodded. "Mage, make it so," he said, and the banshee was whisked away to get on with his new mission.

"Warlock, you do know that he will fail at this once more, correct?" Gelert asked, and his voice was soft as if knowing that testing the warlock could have bad consequences.

"Of course, Gelert. But let's see how he handles his next failure, shall we?" Gonnert said as he smiled.

He got up then and went to the far window, his soft boots making almost no sound on the rock floors of the audience temple room. At the wall, which here in the high tower was an exterior wall, he stopped to look out a loophole window. The loophole windows were often splayed to the inside, enabling archers to hide off to the side while reloading, giving them protection from archers below.

No protection needed now, he knew, but still the narrowness of the window meant that he could see out and across the valley below, but nobody could see him. Green rows of crops with villagers working on their growth lay down below. A road that he could see only a small strip of came over the far hills and toward the castle too, and it held some carts with other harvested goods coming to the castle for trade or sale.

He turned to Gelert and smiled. "We really do have the best spot on the planet, do we not?" he asked, and he motioned for the banshee guarding the door to leave them and close the audience temple door behind him. He sat once again, and his aide perched on the side of the table. "What news from the northern team," he asked.

Gelert grinned at him. "Nothing we didn't already know. Not a single sign of any kind of shipwreck imprint—nor for that matter did they find any kind of telltales in the soil or foliage scans either."

What Gelert didn't say was that once again, Castle Magic was attempting to grow, and that meant they needed new citizens. Finding people to buy in to the magic wasn't a difficult sale, really, as superior technology worked in their favor. No, it was the ability of their society to get past more than eight years of an apocalyptic slide into almost medieval culture and society. The ability of the leaders to both find and bring in those new members was most important.

It had taken a few years to find out all about the treasure from the ship that had come down only a scant few miles away. When they discovered what the ship held, what the Boathi probably called normal technology, it was so superior to anything on Ceti4 that it looked like magic to them at first. As they realized that they too could use the same technology, it meant more to their citizens.

Magic was what it looked like—that's what they said—and as it looked like there was no other explanation, magic was what it was.

They had found the ship more than eleven years ago; the Boathi explorer ship had come down on a glide path that gave little impression that it was going to survive. It had hit the forest near the large open pit beryl mines to the east of the city, and then as it fell into the vast pit, it buried itself in the pit wall like a corkscrew going in deep.

Many had been killed that day.

Many more had died in the early investigations when they had tried to shovel the ship out—they'd only ever gotten a section of the rear of the ship clear enough to gain access. Keeping it secret had been easier than one might think, he knew, as the explanation that there had been a terrible explosion seemed to work well at first. Later, they'd cordoned off the whole beryl mine as they shut it down, and all the workers were laid off or moved to other mines in new areas.

The ship was hidden from others for the most part. They understood innately that owning such a wreck might be advantageous to them all. It had taken years to fully find and understand enough about the technology to enable them to use what few items they had had success with at first.

"The silver belts were one thing that had come pretty easy," he said to himself as he softly caressed the large purple buckle at his waist. Knowing how it worked was a problem they'd yet to solve, but it worked each and every time, which was important.

On a set of pads in what they called the transport room in the ship, they could send out as many as twelve citizens at once to a previously picked location via the console. Thank God, for the Boathi belief in archiving how the transport worked, he thought and grinned. No matter where they were outside of the ship, all they had to do was stand close together and each click the transport button on the rear of the purple buckle at the same time to come home—back to the ship.

It worked. It made Castle Black the home of magic, and while it was a sham, it worked. Few knew the secret of the technology, and all their citizens below the rank of mage thought it to be magic.

Each year, there was a ceremony where some of the banshees were promoted to Mages. And it was then that they learned the explanations behind what their magic really was. The revelation was met with surprise, yet it worked to ensure the chosen few matured into knowing leaders.

He smiled once more and thought about the latest reports about how to get the second button on the back of the purple belt to work. This button gave the belt wearer a shield against all attacks. The Boathi archives on that included a tutorial too, and he was waiting for that report and vid soon.

Until then, it was magic, and shortly, he and his leaders would possess this magic too. He grinned and felt not a single bit of anxiety at fooling the thousands of Castle Magic citizens.

We do what works … he thought.

#####

Approaching a new planet was always something the Boathi captain enjoyed. No matter if it was his first trip or his fiftieth trip—coming out of FTL and seeing their destination lying before them always gave him an optimistic outlook on the rest of his day.

Ceti4 was the next planet they had to work on—following Boathi Supreme Commands' exacting orders for scans. It had taken almost a full month to deal with the previous planet, and this one was similar in size and continent spreads, so it'd take about the same length of time too. A month of scans using the AI grid pattern would be first and then all the follow-ups when they hit a target that could be the Drake. There would be a month of waiting for the final report, which would be sent to the Boathi home w0rld for them to okay the destruction of power-generating locations all across the planet.

As his dewclaw rasped against his jaw for a moment, he thought about how long it'd been since they'd been back on Boathi. They had been sent out almost a full year ago on this audit of worlds they'd bombed almost a decade ago now. The ship and its crew knew this would be a long mission. He sighed. It was summer back on Boathi, and there would be enormous migrations of the herds of prey on the planet's plains. He loved this time of year and the hunts so much—running and cutting an animal out of the pack and then the killing and eating of fresh meat. Their race had long since moved on from such predator-prey hunts, and the only way one could hunt was to participate in the annual historical hunts held by various factions back on Boathi. As a sphere ship captain, he had been able to get into one of the poshest of such groups, and by his reckoning, the hunts would happen in just a month or so.

Instead of running down a meal, he'd be sitting in this chair, watching the ship's AI record yet another of the interminable grid patterns, report that it found no ship at all, and then move on on to another pattern.

He looked over at the planet that lay below and said to his helmsman, "Plot the most economical grid pattern, time-wise, I mean, and let's get started."

The sub-alternate gave an acknowledgment back, and the view-screen showed that the *Sophon* moved in toward the planet quickly, curving on a run that would take it to the night side first for initial power generating scans. It was a quick drop down and into the atmosphere, and then the AI chimed that it was now plotting a grid pattern.

"Belay that grid pattern—just use the lights we find," the captain said, hoping to get Ceti4 done as quickly as possible. If we can get this one done and it's negative, I can use the lack of any kind of findings on the first run through of all the planets and now the second one of the more detailed grid

scans shows nothing—and take that back to Boathi
to present in person.

Boathi did not grin as a part of their nature, but
the sound of his leg bouncing on the bridge decking
was about the same thing, and he could almost feel
the grass and soil beneath his feet as he hunted for
prey in a month's time.

That might be the most plausible way to get out
of this mission with no chance of success. Where
the Drake had gone was out of his control—and he
knew he'd have a chance explaining that in person
back on Boathi, instead of watching the *Sophon* go
grid by grid over the full list of planets they'd
already searched and found empty.

He stopped his leg from doing its dance on the
bridge deck, and instead, he watched the view-
screen as the terminator went by, and they were
plunged into darkness once again over Ceti4.

"Keep her up at, say, thirty thousand feet,
Helm," he ordered, and the as the darkness below
them dropped away, the few lights grew smaller
too.

The *Sophon* flew on a straight-line grid, section by
section, area by area, region by region, taking its
time and slowing sometimes over larger pools of
lights. Some were plain fires of large villages, while
once in a long while, there was electrical power
lighting a small town or city. Using the map in the

Boathi archives of what had been bombed that decade or so ago, they also visited the old power generating centers too. From what they could detect, there were not many that had been rebuilt or even jury-rigged to still make power, but in a few cases, they made location saves to come back in the daytime to see a bit more clearly.

The sub-alternate spoke up. "Captain, on the sidebar, I have added the list of possibles, and when we find more, that list will be updated," he said.

The captain noted same, added that list to his console display, and settled in for a long, long shift of traversing the planet, grid by grid. Every once in a while, his clawed foot bounced on the bridge deck as he daydreamed of the hunt.

CHAPTER FOUR

As Zoe flew along the coast, mostly everyone was on the port side of the floater, looking down at the waves as they met the shore. About twenty miles back, the big waves had crashed against sand bluffs, and it was an impressive sight to see.

"More erosion than I expected," Toby said. "Guess the waves have been eroding the shoreline with more vigor the past few years. We used to take a floater out to the deep water mobile offshore drilling units, or MODUs we used to call them, and set down to take off personnel and such.

"It was pretty easy work actually, but then along came the Boathi, and most of those MODUs were destroyed when the bombs fell. Seems they couldn't leave our rigs out there, full of oil at all, even though they'd already bombed all the oil tankers that lay moored in cities like Lindos and Shorecroft too," he said as he shook his head.

"Lost lotsa friends back then, so would love to try to even the score somehow."

"When the Forest Empire cult had you fly, you ever come down this way?" Sue asked.

Toby shook his head no. "Not ever—we did, however, try to find some of the northern platform MODUs, but no luck. Even sat above the exact GPS coordinates, and there was nothing down there but water," he said, his voice sad, and he shrugged.

"But," Vera asked, "were there none of these MODUs that did survive?"

He shook his head. "Not as far as I know—course there were hundreds of them all over Ceti4—in the continental shelf areas, mind you. Surely, the Boathi didn't bomb them all, we thought, but we found not a single one of the five we looked for north of here. Waves is all we found, and I shudder to think what kind of death our workers went through back then too."

That quieted the whole seating area, and eyes went back out and down to the shoreline ahead. Bixby snored beside Javor, and he inched a foot under the dog's hip to give him a small prod, but the dog snored on.

The cliffs here were of gray stone about fifty to

one hundred feet in height. The cliffs had been weathered for eons it looked like, and swirling over them were thousands of birds all nesting it appeared on those rock cliffs. Well below them, Javor thought, but still, if Zoe's thrust engines took in one of those birds, it'd be hell on the turbines within. Toby kept them up and well above the threat of bird-strike, and ahead they could see an upcoming large bay with anchorage within that looked populated with some ships.

"Shorecroft lies ahead," Jon said proudly, and he began to call out various city landmarks. "That big red-roofed building on the shoreline is the old federal barracks—now it's run by the Shorecroft Patrol HQ—us, I'd guess.

"Inside the loop of that road, see those low buildings? They're training and barracks and classrooms for our new patrol recruits. Over to the right ahead lies the city itself," he said as he rose up against the window and pointed off to his right.

"Down there is the city center with its admin buildings, city hall, and that big shopping complex too. Bought many a beer there myself over the past too.

"See the LRT moving along? It was re-commissioned just a year ago or so, and we're proud that we got her back up and running too. Only takes like twenty minutes of run time to cross the whole city, but it's a great way to get around in town.

"See the large gray stone buildings off to the side there, past the big green park? That's the university —and it's up and running too once again. Boathi may have bombed us pretty good, but we're making headway into returning to where we were," he said.

Vera nodded at him and clapped him on the shoulder. "Jon, Shorecroft is showing us that we Cetians can't be kept down after the Boathi attacked us. We'd be proud to have you become a larger part of the Regime too," she said.

He smiled at her. "And yes, our first stop will be —if it's okay with you, Vera—at the Patrol HQ, if that's okay?"

She agreed and Toby prepared to swing Zoe around into the wind to come down just beside the building in the large training park area inside the loop of road that now lay just ahead.

Down on the ground, groups of patrollers were gathering and pointing up at the floater. It was the first they'd seen in years, and the surprise was a big one for many there. As Zoe's nose swung back to point somewhat north by northwest, the floater lowered and lowered, and soon it lay just feet off the ground.

Jon and his patrollers were already down on the landing deck, and as the ramp dropped down to the grass, he was the first out the door and began barking orders at some of the patrol recruits who were standing around staring with open mouths.

"You three, run over to the quartermaster, and I want ropes back here—two hundred feet long—and at least five of same back here in less than a minute. You bunch, take a hold of these side sheets, and hold the ship down. She might buck a little every once in awhile if the wind gets under her chin, and you'll be what holds her down. Step to it, cadets," he barked, and around him, there was a sudden scurrying of camouflaged uniforms as they all sprung to action.

A Jeep was drilling at them quickly from across the training area, and as it pulled up, Jon came to attention and saluted with a snap.

"Colonel on deck, TEN-SHUN," he barked, and he, Rick, and Kyle saluted with a snap.

"Sir, Captain Jon Adams, reporting in," he said, and that got him a salute back from the colonel who stepped out of the Jeep.

The colonel was a big man with snow-white hair and wore a very neatly pressed uniform. His face looked like he'd seen it all, Javor thought, as he stepped in closer to Jon and grinned at him.

"Captain, when you said you'd be here in less than a day, there were some over at HQ that laughed—hell, they're still laughing. But like me, they should have never doubted you, Jon," he said, and he threw out a hand to shake.

Jon grinned back and shook his hand, and they all talked at once and laughed too.

The colonel looked at the rest of the group who had come down the landing ramp, and said, "And where is Sandy, lad?"

Jon's face fell for a second, and then he squared his shoulders. "Sir, we lost Sandy—river accident months back, Sir, and we are all still shaken up by that," he said quietly.

That threw a blanket over the welcome for sure, Javor thought as he stepped up to meet the colonel.

"Sir, my name is Javor Novak—and may I introduce Vera Lancaster of the Regime government here on Ceti4, Sir?" he said, taking the bull by the horns. If you wish to break up an awkward moment, divert attention to something else, he thought, and he knew it always worked. And it worked this time as well, as the colonel looked at him first but then at Vera.

"Ma'am—you are known by many of us here in Shorecroft as the head of the Regime—and it's nice to have a visit as well," he said, and he took her proffered hand and shook it heartily.

"I am the past head of the Regime, Colonel— now the new ambassador to Shorecroft—and I have an offer from the Regime to relay to your own government administration, Colonel …?"

He smiled at her. "I am Colonel Nathan Auckland of the Shorecroft Patrol. Jon, here, is in my own regiment, and we have been friends since he tripped me to win an obstacle course training run, what, a dozen years ago," he said.

Javor noted that Jon's hand came up quickly to cover his face, but a smile still crept out.

Vera tipped her head at the colonel. "Thank you for the full introduction—and a side note. Jon is still able to surprise our enemies when he's out in the field too, so it's no surprise his friends get similar surprises too!"

Jon took the ribbing, and they all walked over to the side of the Jeep.

"Sir," the corporal at the wheel said, "I took the liberty of calling for a personnel carrier, and it should be here—he looked back over his left shoulder—"in minutes, Sir."

The colonel nodded and the conversation went on between him and Vera, and Javor noted that no one butted in.

As the personnel carrier moved up to take a flanking position, all of them climbed aboard. The colonel too clambered aboard and sat at Vera's side still deep in conversation.

#####

Black Mage Gelert smiled at the girl and noted she'd almost recovered from the transport. "Yes, I know well the feeling of being transported from one location hundreds of miles to a new one. What just happened to you less than an hour ago was just that —so your stomach will be all a-flutter and your nerves will be pulsing too. We all feel that—but once it happens a few more times, like the rest of us, the feelings get less severe and taper off quickly," he said.

She stared at him, her blonde hair long and swept across a shoulder to hang at her side. Bright sky blue eyes stared back at him. Her face was without a blemish or a mark with one small dimple on her right cheek, and her tiny cleft chin still shook from the transport to Castle Magic.

She was, he thought, *quite beautiful, and yet for some reason he couldn't fathom, she looked somehow incomplete. He had no idea what that meant really, but then he had never met the girl before.*

"You can settle in here and become a part of our own castle group—you will be our new sorceress," he said, keeping the real truth from her.

She nodded.

Good, he thought, *she is at least following along now.*

He waved at the banshee over at the door who came over in a rush. "Banshee, please take our new sorceress over to her new quarters in the dark tower. Make sure that she has the maids there bathe her and give her new clothes too. Also, explain our normal routines to her as well, and then make sure that they know to bring her this evening to the big gala dinner too. You will sit," he said, turning back to the girl, "beside me and the warlock too—a place of honor," he said as he smiled at her.

Moments later the banshee had taken her and led her off, and he realized he didn't even know her name, but that was not so important to him; after all, knowing the name of the sacrificial lamb wasn't important to anyone he remembered from his history.

He worked hard on reports for the rest of the afternoon and was nodding to himself that, yes, he'd been right when he had said to the warlock that Banshee Gillead would be hard-pressed to talk any tribes into becoming citizens of the castle.

Only real way to do that, he knew, was to amaze them with magic—that seemed to make them bow first and ask questions much, much later. If only they knew, he thought and finished yet another report with poor outcomes of new citizens.

At almost dinnertime, a banshee knocked on his door ,and he left the stack of reports half-done but with a smile.

Tonight's dinner was a big deal for the citizens of the castle, as a handful of banshees would be moving up to become full mages in their order. Closed off for the first part of the promotional presentation, the huge gala dining room would then be filled with those lucky enough to have received tickets, and the big dinner party was their reward.

He smiled. *Most of the banshees were shell-shocked. They had no idea that the magic was not at all magical — that in fact it was simply stolen Boathi technology — and that had made him laugh loudly four years earlier when he'd made the promotions list.*

As he walked toward the great hall, he noted there were dozens and dozens of reapers working hard on getting the crowds to all line up in neat orderly rows. With more than a thousand guests here tonight, he knew it was a big deal, but all the Castle Magic citizens expected it every year. The guests expected something spectacular ending with the big event topper itself — the sacrifice of the virgin.

He smiled at that. *The story of the magic needed some kind of grassroots hold on their citizens, he'd been told, and hence the virgin sacrifice that happened every year at this event. He wondered who had ever countenanced such a price to get followers to believe, and then he shrugged it away. As long as the citizens believed in magic, the society was safe.*

He went through the massive four-door doorway and walked the hundred yards or so toward the far head table. Other banshees were there looking after the special tables at the front of the room, and he looked at the head tables, all dressed in pure white, left for the prayer leader too.

He nodded to a banshee he knew a bit, walked around the close end of the head table, and took the stairs at the side to join others already seated at their places. He smiled and talked for a moment with a few of his peers as he walked along behind the seats and eventually made it to the center of the head table.

He took a moment to chat with the only girl at the table, and he smiled at her too. She was nice, but he knew that didn't matter a whit, and he nodded at whatever she said and then moved past the next two empty chairs to take his seat at the right-hand side of the head table. Her title for the past year had been sorceress, but that was about to change.

One of those empty chairs would soon hold the warlock, and the last empty chair would hold the newly acquired blonde virgin he'd seen just hours ago.

Music was struck up, and the sounds filled the almost empty hall as the soon-to-be promoted banshees were led in by two ceremonial mages, dressed in red robes, to take their single table in front of the head table.

They sat and the music suddenly changed to a loud fanfare, and the warlock appeared down off to one side, coming in from a private entrance. He walked right past the empty tables and eventually made his way to the rear of the head table to climb the stairs and seat himself at the center chair.

He nodded to them all and said to his black mage, "Begin, Mage Gelert."

He rose and motioned for the ceremonial red-robed mages to begin.

They rose from the table in front of him and had the banshees leave their seats and stand in a straight line in front of the warlock, who rose and began to explain to them the real truth behind Castle Magic.

"We are not magicians. Not a single thing that you have been led to believe is done with magic. Yes, I know, you're thinking of how with your own eyes, you've seen people disappear, have seen them be impervious to attack, and how a simple wave of a wand can kill. That is all true, but as full mages here in our society, you must know now—this is not magic but simple technology. Technology that we stole from the Boathi," he said.

Among the handful of banshees standing in front of him were questioning faces and small head shakes. One even said, "Not really!"

The warlock turned to one of his red-robed mages and said, "Show us the belts."

The man went over to a side table. From under a cloth there, he took up a thin silver belt, which he held up for all of the banshees to see.

The warlock said, "You know about these belts, you all wear similar belts—but what you did not know is that when your own personal belt is turned on by us, it has powers you never knew about. Show us, Mage."

The red-robed mage showed his belt that he was wearing, reached down to the big purple crystal buckle, and made a small adjustment to same. Another red-robed mage stood to his left about ten feet away and pointed at him with a short foot-long black tube—a wand, they all called them.

From the wand, a hiss was heard, and the mage facing the wand was fine. He smiled at the banshees and held up his hand as if to say "see, I'm fine."

The warlock continued. "Our belts, when turned on, provide complete protection from any kind of missile, arrow, bullet, or weapon. They do not provide, however, protection against gravity or inertia—if you jump off a cliff with the belt turned on, you will still die. But, as you can see, they will protect us … and now as full mages, your own belts have just been turned on. You are now mages in Castle Magic," he said as he finished and sat.

Beside him, Mage Gelert still stood and looked at the new mages before him. "Yes, I know, you've tons of questions. All can wait until tomorrow until your first audience with the warlock. For tonight, all you now need to do is to learn how to turn your belt off later, and then enjoy the congratulations of the citizens who will be allowed into the room in a few minutes. But we do have one more ceremony to take on this evening. May I ask, please, that our sorceress please join the new mages in front of the head table?

The girl smiled, rose, went down the rear stairs to come around to the front of the head table, and joined the group of mages now all in a row again. She took a spot at the far left side of the line and smiled at them all.

From the side, the prayer leader had made his way forward and now stood in front of the line of new mages. He held up his hands to the ceiling way above them all, as they bowed their heads in prayer.

He began to make a small chanting set of sounds that slowly grew in volume. His hands fell to his sides as he bent over at his waist to reach forward and touch the ground, emphasizing all with his chant.

As he rose up, one hand now held the same wand that the mages had held, and he swept it across the whole line from his right to his left. Not a single mage was affected, of course, as they were all wearing their belts; however, the sorceress gasped once, fell to her knees, and then slumped over, now dying on the floor.

The mages to her left were shocked.

The prayer leader said, "We have sacrificed to our own gods what was pure and untouched by both man and Boathi too. We do this to show that while technology plays a major role in our society, we do not forget our gods. We do this every year on this date, and now as full mages, you are charged with the duty to know this—and to keep it secret from the next sorceress too." He turned on his heel and walked off toward the far wall.

Black Mage Gelert smiled at them all, still standing, as the two red-robed mages picked up the body of the sorceress, and they followed the prayer leader way off to their left.

"Sit now, please, Mages. Banshees, open the doors and let's let our guests in. Congratulations to our new mages who now know all of the Castle Magic secrets to keep secure for the rest of their lives," he said as he too sat.

The noise in the room increased as the hordes of guests went to their tables to sit, then dine, and then party. As the hordes slowly got settled and then looked at the head table, the warlock chose to wait a few more minutes and then smiled at them all as he rose.

"We, the leaders of Castle Magic, welcome you

all to our annual gala promotion dinner. We have new mages," he said as he had them rise and turn to face the crowds behind them, and the cheering was loud and long.

"We thank you for your attendance here and we have—as you all know—only one more duty to perform this evening, to introduce our new sorceress. Sorceress Jennifer will be her name," he said as he waved off to his left.

On the far wall, a door opened and the new sorceress entered the room timidly. She was immediately met by the prayer leader who led her all the way to the back of the head table and helped her up the stairs to take her place to the right of the warlock.

She smiled shyly when cheers went up in the room, and she nodded to her right at the black mage who grinned back at her. She was the new sorceress, and she would help rule for a year.

#####

Vera began the conversation, and from what Javor knew and could follow, when it came to making a pitch, she was good. She began—as all things did—with the Boathi incursions and bombings of almost a decade ago.

"We lost just about everything with no guilt on our own part at all. The Human Empire was losing the war with the Boathi, and while it was not the best thing that ever happened to Ceti4—it surely was better than being taken over for full Boathi colonization," she said, her voice spitting out the enemy's name.

"We have come back too, a long, long way. In the Regime, we have power from over a dozen power-generating stations—a few wind, one solar, and still we use hydro dams to get power to the grid. We have fully covered our tracks too, in that all of the smaller sub-stations and transfer points are underground and hidden. We have also launched new manufacturing to begin to replace that which we lost those years ago. Farming is back and in full swing. Our Regime government is doing all that it can to help our citizens with the normal flux of trying to live in this post-Boathi world. Bones is what we call Ceti4 now—as the skeleton of what they didn't destroy is still enough of a foundation to begin again."

She smiled at the four of the people across the table from her who were at this first meeting to discuss the Regime and its presentation to Shorecroft. They were elected officials—Javor knew that being such might be problematic as all elected officials were interested in one thing only—getting re-elected. But these four seemed to be truly honest in their approach to the issue of becoming a part of the Regime.

One of them, the woman in the foursome, had asked about family life. Children. Schools. Parks. Higher education too, as if she was weighing the future of the Regime based on its current treatment of its citizens who were family based. Vera had been honest and was proud to say that just last year, the first graduation class at the Arlington University since the bombing had been convocated, and she was proud of the new college graduates. The woman, named Judy, Javor thought, if his memory served, asked for more though.

"Vera, one graduating class is a great sign that the Regime is making progress at bringing our society back to normal—but what about the Regime itself? You are not elected officials—in fact, if anything, you are all a group of dictators," she said.

That caused a bit, at least in Javor's mind, of awkward silence, but Vera nodded and held up a hand to counter the question.

"Agreed—we did take on the roles of running the Regime, but instead of elections, we used the move-through-the-chairs system. Each of the seven of us was asked to join, one per year. Each moves through the various ministries and areas of society management, moving up a seat if you will. Until the member's seventh year, when they move up to be the head of the Regime leaders group. I was in that position myself just last year—and now I'm no longer a member of the leaders at all—I'm an ambassador now to Shorecroft," she said, and that got some nods at the table.

Behind her, seated in a few rows of chairs, the rest of the team from the Regime sat and watched the proceedings with calmness and polite attention. Wayne was playing with something, but a nudge from Bruce made him stop. Jessica was still long in the face with sadness over her sister, but she knew that soon they'd make an attempt at getting her—at least that's what she'd been promised. Toby was all smiles though as he'd been able to get some more fuel from the Shorecroft Patrol stores and had learned that over off the island to the south, called Nancy Island, there was still a standing oil platform. No one had known if it was still populated or a working oil platform, but Toby knew a quick trip to same was on their future mission list too. Jon and his patrollers, Rick and Kyle, were also seated but in a row that was behind the four leaders of Shorecroft as the representatives of the patrol, along with Colonel Auckland, who had met them in person. The last member of the group was Bixby who was lolling on his side, breathing heavy as he must have been hot. City hall was a big and impressive building, but the power that Shorecroft had at its use obviously didn't include running any kind of air conditioning, as the room was hot and the air static.

Bixby says it all, Javor thought.

Happy group though, Javor thought as he scraped the edge of his thumbnail along the side seam of his pants. An edge on the nail caught on the seam, and it made him think that the smallest of things could sometimes cause an issue. Perhaps, he thought, the thumbnail was talking to him, but he shook that off as the foursome all gathered their heads together to chat privately.

Shortly thereafter, one of the men, dressed as they all were in camouflage gear clothing, nodded and then leaned back in his chair. "We understand what it is the Regime is offering—and let me paraphrase it once for the record. That if Shorecroft wishes to become a part of the Regime, we may do so. We would be a full state as you offered," he said as he pointed to the printed presentation folder Vera had tendered hours earlier, "and that would mean that we would get a seat on the Regime council. We would get for our own population, full citizenship in the Regime—every man, woman, and child. We would also get access to your own full power grid, your manufacturing products and assets, and perhaps, most importantly, we would be a full voting state member."

He leaned forward toward Vera. "Do I have that

110

correct?" and he got a big nod back as verification from her too.

"This state that we become will need to be—what's the word—governed by someone though, someone who knows us, who has our own interests at heart, and who can act as liaison between Shorecroft and the Regime. We would ask then that that person be our own Colonel Auckland. Military man, lots of service in his past, and he's been an acting mayor for the town for years. Would that be acceptable to the Regime?" he asked.

Vera took only a moment to consider that, and then she answered. "Yes, by all means—Colonel Auckland will be the liaison—but I've something to add to that request. That we at the Regime, with our first state—the Shorecroft state, will also appoint a person to act for the Regime too—and it is going to be our own Sue Fines—right here," she said as she turned in her seat and gestured for her to stand.

Sue stood, a blossom of blush on her cheeks, but she nodded to them at the table and then to the colonel sitting just behind the Shorecroft delegation. "Shorecroft is our first Regime state—so it would be my honor to work with the colonel to help to integrate our two societies and our citizens too, to form a new and lasting union," she said, and that got them all smiling.

Behind the table, the colonel rose too. "It would also be my own honor to work with Sue and the Regime to ensure that the process goes along without any hitches—not that there won't be some. But we will work together to get them all straightened out STAT, and that's my plan."

Vera smiled at the foursome across the table. "We have, as you know, the floater that allows us to move huge distances quickly. We also have been able to get vehicles back on the roads too—trucks at this point only, but that is an ongoing process. As the first state of the Regime, we will teach this to your own people, and you too will soon have transportation that is quicker than hiking."

That too got more smiles, and the talks went on for almost an hour more.

Jon and his group were asked to come back to Shorecroft though as their own mission had been long over, and that made the colonel interject.

"My own idea would be to appoint Jon as the new in-the-field liaison connection between myself and Sue too. I realize that she will be out on Bones a fair bit, and as she and Jon already have history and a relationship that works, then I'd say let's use that for both Shorecroft and the Regime and allow him to be our voice in the field," he said.

That took some thinking and doing, but eventually all at the table agreed to it. Sue and the colonel were to be the liaisons between the Regime and Shorecroft, and Jon would act on Shorecroft's behalf in the field. The colonel added that he'd perhaps like to send along a real squad-sized group of patrollers too, but that could wait.

In less than a half hour, all had been agreed to, and as Vera tendered the radio frequency listings to the table, they were gladly accepted, and the foursome had only a few more questions.

"So, what's next for you, Vera, and your group on the floater," the woman asked.

"We have to go to Maxwell first," Vera replied, "to get some other ducks in a row, and then we thought we'd go north to Castle Magic to see if we can rescue a girl sold into slavery there," she said.

The woman across the table shook her head negatively. "From what little we know about this Castle Magic—is that they can and do have magic. Can't hurt them and they disappear whenever they want to is what little we know. If you're thinking of trying to take her by force, I'd imagine that you are in for a real shock," she said.

From behind her, the colonel spoke up too. "I don't know much more than that—but they all are armed with some kind of a magic wand—that if they wave it over you, you die. That I've seen with my own eyes—a quick and sudden death is what I saw back then. I doubt that our own arms would be any kind of worry to them," he finished off.

Vera nodded. "Yes, but it's Jessica's twin sister," she said as she half-turned to point at the young blonde girl seated behind her, "and we missed our chance in Lindos—so we are going to try once more."

"Jessica and Toby too, of course, sprung our Sue and her squad from the clutches of the Forest Empire—so we owe her the chance to find and free her own sister," she said.

Nods again, Javor noted, and even his own head was nodding too.

After the meeting wrapped up and formal papers were going to be prepared and then signed tomorrow, his team all left the city hall building in the center of town.

The lure of the shopping mall just across the street was large, but instead of joining the shoppers in his crowd, Javor decided to walk back to Zoe, moored a few miles away.

"Time to see what Shorecroft was all about— maybe even go down to the harbor," he said to himself.

Wait, I need to feed Bixby, he thought, and he made his way down the long street toward Zoe who floated in the distance with Bixby trotting at his side.

#####

As Zoe floated along the forests just as they reared up ahead, Toby made some small adjustments to the helm, and she slowly turned to face where they'd come from.

There, close to the edge of the sea, lay Shorecroft, and while it was only a small town in reality, it was quite spread out along the shoreline. They had left only an hour ago, so the town was about seventy miles away, but from here and at this height, it looked closer. From here, only the colors and the general layout could be seen, but Sue had still wanted to turn to look back, and Toby had accommodated her as best he could.

She nodded at Toby and said, "We're about a third of the way between Maxwell and Shorecroft, right?" and that got her an "Aye, Ma'am" back. She smiled at Javor who was seated beside her in the seating area behind the cockpit.

"From here to Maxwell, it's quite a bit of real estate to be responsible for," she said, her voice a bit lower in volume to keep it between just the two of them.

Javor grinned at her. "You'll do fine, Sue—you have the skills to govern this region, and I'm sure of it. So is Vera and Maeve too, so you're covered," he said.

She nodded but she wasn't finished with her

doubts. "But a region with one state—Shorecroft—
is not where it's going to end. I've got to get out
and find others," she said.

He smiled at her. "And yes, I know, there aren't
really many more big towns like Shorecroft to find
and pitch to. But there are others though, like
maybe the tribe we met under the interstate—
remember, the ones that helped save us from those
zombies? Or how about Walkerville too … surely
there's folks there that will come on-board once
their own army base is cleared up of their zombies,
right?" he asked.

Sue nodded and the conversation dried up. Toby
took her okay and turned Zoe to point once again
north by northwest toward Maxwell.

Below them, the plains that ran toward the sea
gave over to the forests that sprung up the farther
north one went. Railway tracks lay below too, but
no trains had ridden them since the Boathi attacks.
The forests that surrounded them were not as thick
as in the far north, and occasionally a regional road
went by and farms could be seen. A gas station well
below had a whole bunch of cars and trucks parked
all around it, and Javor wondered why that might
be, but they cruised over at ten thousand feet, and
there was no real reason to stop to check. At a farm
some miles farther on, there looked like there were
a bunch of people who'd emptied out of the

farmhouse to all stare up and point at Zoe.

Toby offered to make a slower approach to Maxwell and Sue okayed same.

"Better to sneak in low so that we don't attract too much attention," she said, and Toby nodded back his agreement.

Ahead of them, as they got another hour of flying time in, they could see the start of the rolling hills where Maxwell lay with broad ridges of up-swelling rock and trees and deep stark valleys in between. These ridges or small mountains ran from the southwest to the northeast, and as Zoe went over the beginnings of same, most of the evidence of civilization below them disappeared. Raw rock met the sky below, and the colors of reds, oranges, and ochers beneath them was a sight that was well worth the trip.

As Zoe moved on, the floater dropped in altitude, and Javor could see the ridges below slowly growing in size. At one point, they saw a section of the interstate thereof to the northeast, sparsely holding cars and trucks now long unused. A whole section of the roadway was missing, and as he remembered, there was a tribe there they'd met, and he wondered if all was well with them now.

Zoe continued to drop as she now aimed a little more northward, and on the ridge line ahead, now only a few hundred feet below, the shine of the river in the valley appeared. Javor knew Maxwell was just over that ridge, but what he couldn't see was any evidence that the *Drake* had hit the ridge line—shrubs had populated what must have been a wide skid mark as his ship had bounced off the top of the ridge to then fall below it and into the valley.

Sue pointed. "Can't see any evidence that your ship hit at all," she commented and Javor nodded.

As Zoe went over the ridge line and Maxwell lay below, he looked carefully below. Even figuring where the *Drake* lay, as he knew the layout below, he could barely make her out, trapped in the trees and now covered with foliage fresh this year. She was still there though; he could make her out, but to an eye that didn't know where she lay, she was hidden, he thought, and that got a smile.

As Zoe moved now down farther and across the river, Maxwell loomed up in front of them. Once a town of about fifteen thousand souls, it now had less than a thousand. Some lived hidden lives, venturing out only when armed. Others lived life as it had been and avoided all zombies like the plague. Others, like the cadre had been, were trying to help Maxwell out of the doldrums of what had befallen them, and that job was gaining some strength.

Zombies, of course, were a large part of the problem, and while Zoe floated over top of the city, they didn't see any, but no one made the mistake of thinking they weren't still there.

Sue pointed ahead to Toby. "See that large official-looking building—the Maxwell Courthouse? Put her down in the park beside her," she said, and Toby moved the stick and the pedals to accomplish that. In less than twenty more minutes, Wayne and Bruce were down on the landing ramp, tying up the floater, and making her fast.

"What kind of AI is built into this thing?" Vera asked as Toby was going through his shutdown checklist.

"Not much," he replied, "but the normal intruder alert klaxons and a dead-stick result. No one can start her up and take off unless they have the pilot code and enter it in manually. I've got the code—and I gave it to both Jessica and Jon too—would you like it as well?" he asked.

Vera shook her head and said, "Not at all, but I think Sue should have it as well. Once we're landed, do set the intruder AI up, and remember to always do that here in Maxwell."

While Sue was getting a quick lesson in numbers and seeing how to enter that code into the dash, Javor went down with Jon and his patrollers to look around the courthouse. He went across the park street, over the curb, and through the un-tended gardens, which still looked the same.

Bruce had already taken up a spot aimed at the front door, and Wayne was doing a once-over tour of the front of the big stucco building. He went from side to side up the big stairs up to the front porch area and looked at the ground and the concrete from one end to the other. He approached the front door to see it clearly, and after staring at it for a moment, he came back to the top of the stairs to yell down to them all.

"From what I can see, no visitors who left any traces—so no zombies is what I'd guess. Front door still sealed, and the two telltales we left are undisturbed," he finished off.

By now, all of them were on the sidewalk below, and Sue took charge.

"Okay, let's go in, shall we? AI will squawk, but I have the passwords. Anyone have any kind of alien tissue—Javor notwithstanding," she inquired which got her head shakes from all present.

Moments later, with the big front door now open, she walked into the large foyer and went right up to the large AI box that was positioned to the left of the big stairs.

The AI bot had three red lights up at the top, and she spoke slowly and distinctly to it. "AlphaControl —execute stop order one-T-sixty-six," and the three red lights suddenly went out.

She paused as a working sound came from the
bot, and a ray of bright light shot out of the top of
the bot to slowly scan them all in front of the
machine. As the ray moved, it paused on Javor for a
full minute and then moved to finish scanning
everyone else.

Sue smiled. "AlphaControl—please admit all to
full member status. Did you find anything odd,"
she asked, but her tone said that it hadn't as she
knew.

The AI chimed three times, and then a voice said,
"Only the previously authorized alien tissue within
the human named Javor as noted almost nine
months ago originally. AI admits all present as full
members," and the bot chimed three more times as
three green lights were lit up on the top-mounted
display.

Sue grinned. "We're in and fine. Wayne to the
kitchen—we'd like one hell of a meal. Bruce, please
contact our food suppliers, and let them know we're
back and would appreciate anything they can offer
today—but back on regular delivery, please,
starting tomorrow. Vera, please accompany me—all
of you too—up to our second floor, and let's get us
all sorted out for quarters and such," she said, and
they all went upstairs.

CHAPTER FIVE

"Relatively easy," she said to herself, *"is this sorceress role thingy ... at least so far."*

She warned herself not to assume that the few things she'd had to do in her first week were indicative of what lay ahead. She walked on, with what she assumed were her usual retinue, the three banshees who seemed to worship the ground she walked on.

She smiled at the one who had joined her again, walking in step with her at her side. This banshee was a woman named Gisele, just a few years older than she was, and she usually had a big broad smile on her face. They shared the same hair color, that rich blonde shade that shone in the sunshine today, and while she was a foot taller than Jennifer, she bowed her head always to talk to her.

Banshees, Jennifer realized, *were not at the top of the food chain here in Castle Magic. That spot was reserved for the mage class, and they always wore those black robes, gathered at the waist by their signature silver belt with that big ugly purple crystal that was mounted on the belt buckle. Every once in a while, her group would be met by reapers—they appeared to be at the bottom of the food chain and did all the grunt work.*

She grinned at that, thinking *she used to have the same job back in her village—she and her twin Jessica, that was.*

That thought wiped the smile from her face, and she shook her head at Gisele who had laid a hand on her arm to ask if everything was all right.

All right? What could be all right with what she faced and her missing twin?

The fact the slavers had attacked her village, killed too many of her friends, and then taken her sister and her as slaves had not been all right at all. The fact she had been sent down to Lindos by the Forest Empire's prime disciple to be sold once more as a way to split up her and her twin was also not all right. The fact she'd been bought by the Castle Magic black mage and then somehow whisked to the castle using magic was not all right either.

The fact she'd been made this sorceress person was, however, all right.

She had expected that slaves here would be

treated like slaves—put to doing hard manual labor for the good of society. But not so—in fact, as she had been looking for slaves here all week, she'd found none. Not a single one. All the grunt work, as she called it, was done by citizens or reapers in some instances.

Where they were going was not up to her, and she continued walking as Gisele took the lead often to guide her little party. Often, when they'd meet regular citizens, they'd bow from their waists to her, and some even called out "Sorceress … help me," and only Gisele keeping her going had prevented her from stopping to see what she could do.

Ahead at an intersection of the small street within the castle grounds, three people stood in their way, a man, a woman, and a small child. The child, from what she could see, looked ill. The small boy had a very red face, and sweat beaded up on his brow. Even to her own untrained eye, she could see he was in bad shape.

As they approached, Gisele pressed something into her palm and whispered, "Just lay this on the boy's forehead after praying for him—it will make him better."

Banshee Gisele presented her to the father and mother and then stepped aside for them to talk to the sorceress.

"Sorceress Jennifer, we ask that you help us. Our

son, Grayson, has been taken over by some kind of sickness. He cannot eat, his skin is burning up, and only the sorceress can help, we know. Please, please help us …" he said, and he and his wife pushed their small son forward as they bowed from the waist toward her.

She looked down at the boy, cupping the medicine patch so it couldn't be seen, and she knelt to be right in front of the lad. She used what she called her grown-up voice and began to chant.

"Great gods in the sky, I, the sorceress of Castle Magic, ask that you look down on this boy and help us to heal him. To give him back his health and to make him whole again—I ask in your name," she intoned, hoping it sounded okay. She had been taught this just a couple of days back by Gisele as a standard prayer to use when she was trying to help citizens, and she'd gotten it out pretty good, she thought.

As she finished, she wiped the boy's brow with her left hand, back and forth, and then clasped his brow with her right hand, pressing the patch into his skin. She held her hand there as she went on with the prayer.

"Great gods, this is the boy—yes, this is the boy who needs your help and your aid. This is the boy who you will look upon and make whole, great gods …" she finished off and gently pulled her right hand away from his brow. The patch had dissolved already.

As she turned him around to now face his parents, even she could tell he looked a bit better. The redness had already gone down to blush, and he almost smiled up at her as he turned his head back to her.

"Thank you, Sorceress Jennifer," he said, his voice thin and raspy, but she could tell he meant it as his mother gasped and took him up into her arms. The father dropped to his knees, bowed, and kissed the spot that his son had just been standing on.

"Sorceress Jennifer, we thank you for our son's life, and we will say prayers for you at worship tomorrow too," he said over and over.

Gisele nodded to her, and she went into her usual ending speech, having learned it just yesterday.

"Remember, citizens, that Castle Magic is the place where our great gods look down on you, and we would just ask that you live magic lives forever," she said.

The prayer and ending speech made little sense to Jennifer and meant nothing to her. *Applying a medicine to the boy's forehead, disguised as magic of the gods, meant nothing to her either.*

Being a sorceress meant little to her except that she was not doing hard manual labor like pulling those huge stones to build the pyramid in the Forest Empire.

Being the Castle Magic sorceress was not a difficult job—but in fact, one that she could actually do—at least on the surface. She wondered if later today, if she asked Gisele again to explain why things were done this way, if she'd get an answer. She'd asked every day and had gotten no answers she could use. She had also asked about the last sorceress. The answer that she'd been sent north to the castle's new city was somewhat troublesome. Wouldn't a new city be so much rawer than this one, with less in the way of her nice sorceress perks?

Maybe after her bath tonight with the masseuse to apply the oils and the hair girl to help keep her long blonde locks in check, she could get more answers from Gisele. She smiled at Gisele, and they left the family still bowing and calling her name in thanks.

#####

Wayne was out tending the gardens in the back; the months they'd been gone had been tough on them, and many of the beds were overgrown with weeds and undergrowth. Javor stood and watched a bit, and then he helped by pulling out some of the larger weeds.

Wayne nodded and pointed to his right. "See the sage plants here—Jimmy was so proud he got them to take and really do well—and now they're all overrun by these damn weeds," he said. He didn't mean to, but all of a sudden, his face welled up.

"Jimmy ... good God, I'd forgotten ..." he said with fervor. "May he rest in peace, I'd hope," and he turned away from Javor to forcefully yank out more weeds.

Javor didn't mention their dead companion and methodically just pulled out the weeds to lay them in a large pile that Wayne had started to build. They worked for over an hour at that, getting the spice beds back and looking much healthier than they'd been for months. Finally, the four large beds looked much better, and he said quietly to Wayne, "Looks better, eh?"

Wayne nodded back to him and swept a hand across the whole garden. "Sure does, Javor, thanks for the help. We'll have some spices now for our dinner—it's gonna be a fish fry as I've got some frozen fillets available, and our fresh food delivery doesn't start until tomorrow," he said.

He plucked some of the tarragon and rosemary.

"Tarragon butter and mustard sauce over the whitefish that I'll bread first before sautéing same." He grinned and Javor's taste buds watered. If there was one thing that was true here on Bones, it was that humans still enjoyed their food, and while he'd eaten too many MREs, the dinners that he'd enjoyed were ranked right up there in his mind.

Javor and Wayne went back into the courthouse, and they mounted the steps up to the second floor area where some of the others sat talking. Javor almost placed the box of fillets on the counter, and Wayne motioned him to take it into the kitchen off to the side, and he did that instead. When he came back out, Vera and Sue were in a very pointed chat.

"And I think it's the wrong thing to do—sorry, Jessica, but I think that for us to just go to this Castle Magic and see if we can get your sister is looking for trouble," Vera said.

Sue nodded but then answered on behalf of the entire group who had been slaves up in the Forest Empire. They had for weeks and weeks pulled those heavy stones up the pyramid, being whipped and berated for not being strong enough. They'd been treated like slaves—they were just that, slaves in the Forest Empire world, and that too had been hard to swallow for free men and women.

"We owe our freedom to many people who helped us escape. Javor held the Empire's prime disciple at spear point, allowing Toby and Jessica to spring us out on the floater. We owe many—and for Jessica, all she has asked is to get our help to free her sister. Her sister who is now a slave in Castle

Magic. We really have no choice in that matter, Vera, now do we?" she questioned.

Before Vera could even answer, Jessica, who'd come in from the rear hallway where the bedrooms were, interrupted.

"Vera, Sue, and all of you. My twin and I lived a simple life as villagers in the forest, and we know that we would have been more than happy to have lived that life. Yet somehow, life intervened—we were taken by attackers on our village. Many died that day but we—most likely as we were twins, we thought—were sold into slavery to the Forest Empire.

"Why I was sent to pull stones and she was not, I do not know—but seeing her being sold a second time in Lindos meant that she was no longer property of the Forest Empire—so yes, I do ask and implore you to help me free her from slavery in Castle Magic. It's all I'd ever ask … and with Zoe, we can be there in less than a day and a bit and then home again back here to Maxwell."

Vera toyed with her spoon; it clinked against the side of her cup a few times as she pondered that.

Javor spoke up. "With superior firepower and ordnance that I can provide from the *Drake* armory, I'd say we've a top-notch chance to get her out of this castle," he offered.

Vera looked at him, her eyes weighing her

options. No longer the head of the Regime, she still carried a lot of weight with the current leaders. She knew that the final word would be hers.

She nodded at Jessica. "We will see what Javor can help us with, arms-wise, and then let's plan a trip to Castle Magic for the end of the week. Sue, I thought you were going to see if you can get some of the local tribes involved too—have you a timeline for that?"

Sue smiled. "Soon as Jennifer is back here no longer a slave, we'll go to the interstate and look them up once more and see what they say," she said.

"Then I'd say let's relax for a couple of days, and head to Castle Magic three days from today," Vera said, which got nods all around.

As he went down the corridor on the deck for his quarters, the Boathi captain was still somewhat frustrated.

The hunt back on Boathi Prime was going to start in less than twenty days, and here he was on a mission with little chance of success. The fact that it would go on for at least five more months of fruitless grid searches over five more planets was the main reason for his displeasure.

He stopped partway down the corridor, leaned

on a door jamb, and reached down to scratch his shin with his claws. "Itch gone," he said to himself as he straightened and continued toward the lift.

As he clicked the button on the door, he suddenly wondered *why no one had ever made the ship's AI look after the lifts and done away with the button. Would be easier, he thought, to just have to say I want to go to the bridge deck than to push a button here on the outside of the lift and then again inside to denote which deck to go to.*

That could wait for another day, and he waited, as the sounds from the lift in front of him grew closer. Once inside, he pushed the bridge deck button, and the lift door slid closed. As the lift went up, he felt it slide sideways too, as the sphere ship provided full access to all decks, both horizontally and vertically.

Moments later, his frustration still not appeased, the door slid open, and he was on the bridge. He took his captain's seat with a thump. The thump was noted by all of the bridge crew too, and he asked for an update. "Sub-alternate, your report, please," he said firmly.

Ahead of him, a Boathi half-turned to face him and nodded. "Captain, we are about twenty percent done with the scans on this continent. We have found nothing at this point—but we continue to see and note that the humans below have come back strongly with their new power generation. Some cities—well, few really—have full power including lights, residential and commercial and manufacturing power, public transit powered by hydro-power as well. The humans appear to be rebounding from our attacks of more than eight years ago, Captain," he said.

Damn. The captain didn't want to hear this on top of the lack of finding the human ship, and he said so. "Sub-alternate, find the ship. That's what I want. A few bombs will put these human cities back into the stone age, so take those worries off your plate and find me that ship!" he said, his voice cruel, and he leaned forward to emphasize his anger.

The sub-alternate again nodded, said, "Aye, Captain," and turned back to face the big view-screen.

Twenty thousand feet below them, the terrain flew by slowly as the *Sophon* cruised on its grid pattern. Forests, lakes, and rivers were interspersed with small towns and farms, most of which looked unattended. There was a fire in one of the forests ahead that was moving slowly downwind toward them, and the captain hoped it'd burn the whole continent down, but he knew it would not.

As the *Sophon* flew on, the bridge was silent as usual, and all eyes were on the ground below. On the left side of the view-screen lay a display with the grid pattern itself. Some of the lines of the squares were colored bright pink for the areas yet to be covered, and others were jet-black for areas already searched.

According to the ship's AI, the pink lines were the ones that had to be followed and scanned from above. He'd belayed that order more than four days ago, and still the *Sophon* had found nothing. The pink grid lines that had been skipped were flashing on the display to remind anyone looking that that those areas had not been searched. Instead, the *Sophon* had used the nighttime scans of lights to determine where power was being used and then had done full scans on those centers—big or small.

It had, as yet, produced no indication of a human ship.

And still those pink grid lines flashed at him.

There were still far more pink lines left than I want, the captain thought, *and then there was that whole northern continent to search, islands too,* and he knew the *Sophon* would be here on Ceti4 for still weeks and weeks.

If he wished to make a stand and give up on the search for the human ship, he'd need to make his decision in less than ten days. That would give him enough time to come up with a plausible story on their FTL flight back to Boathi Prime, in time to

still join the hunt. That's if he thought the idea
would work; otherwise, he'd be sitting here
watching pink lines flash.

*So much for my hunt. So much for the thrill of the
chase and matching strides with a quarry as I run down
my prey.*

His clawed foot bounced on the bridge deck as he
daydreamed of the hunt.

#####

As the crew of dumb-now-smarter zombies
headed back to their barracks, the team leader half-
smiled to his smart zombie helper.

"So, while they are not what I'd call real workers,
they can—if not properly watched and guided—
totally mess up just about any job," he said,
exasperatedly.

Shelagh nodded. Two smart zombies led each of
the enhanced zombie teams, and she grinned back
at Fred.

"Fred, if it's one thing we all know, it's that a bite
from us gives the dumb-now-smarter zombie some
kind of smarts—but not enough to understand any
kind of planning. Or construction. Or even how to
eat with a knife and fork," she said, and that made
them both laugh.

The Walkerville Army Base had been
undergoing some major changes, and their team

had been one of the five teams asked to help with construction of security features that would seriously impede any more attacks. The base itself, with more than four miles of fence around it, had been walked and fence breaches noted. It was their team's job to knit in new wire for the frost-wire fencing to make the links whole again.

They'd worked hard for most of the day and had cleaned up their work area—well, cleaned up was what the dumb-now-smarter zombies might say they did. Fred thought throwing all the tools into a bin and leaving the rolls of wire fencing still lying on the grass was barely a cleanup, but then he was just the team leader.

Fred smiled as they followed the dozen or so workers in their party back across the large grass swath that lay behind the rows of barracks buildings. On their left still lay the huge sewer pipes that had once been stacked up for future use —now lying askew and almost overgrown with underbrush. Months ago, an attack force had bombed that stack of pipes that had some zombie snipers in same—and the resulting fires and death toll had been overwhelming. Now the pipes were blackened from the fire that had raged, and the blackened drill field grass had remained black, but now he could see the first evidence of new growth pushing up from the black fire residues. A few pipes were stuck in the ground on angles, and one had also been jammed into a long buried culvert that went out of the base underground and over to the ditch on the far side of the road. They only knew that because of the influx of raccoons and other scavengers that used this route to gain access to the base without being stopped by the tall boundary fence. It was on Fred's list to fill up that sewer pipe to seal out any of these scavengers, and he sighed, knowing it'd be a few days of digging up soil and filling up the pipe. Hard digging, and he'd want to get more bitten zombies for that, and he made a note to ask for same.

The grass had once been cared for and trimmed, but it now was almost thigh-high with shoots of weeds and broken limbs of trees that ran along the frost-wire outer fence. The hundred or so yards of what had once been well-tended drill fields were well past their best before date, Fred thought as he tramped along.

Shelagh was a great help though, he realized.

Before the Boathi had bombed the planet, she had been an administrative assistant to some high mucky-muck in the insurance business sector, so while knitting new fence into old broken fence was something she knew little about, she had the dumb zombies down cold. She'd gotten them to listen and to pay attention, and once Fred had shown them how to measure and cut a new piece of the frost-wire fencing replacement coil, she had been able to help them see how to stitch it in. How to lock it tight. How to use the pliers and the wrenches to make sure the hole that had been there was now permanently sealed up.

The fact that the measuring seemed to be beyond them at all was no real surprise, so Fred did that. And then he had Shelagh supervise the cutting of the new pieces. It worked. It was neither fast nor efficient, he thought, but then could anything using dumb zombies be anything like that.

As they slowly made their way across the drill field, another team came in along the road off to their right. The dumb zombies led and were followed by the smart zombie leaders.

Fred waved at them and caught up with them. "Sam, how'd it go today?" he inquired. a

Sam grinned. "Running a team of dummies is like not what I expected to do. Day after the bombs fell and I came to, I knew I'd changed ... but good God, these creatures are like almost un-coachable," he said, shaking his head.

Fred knew too. Just the coming to that Sam had mentioned meant something as 99.9% of the humans on Ceti4 had not come to—they'd died in the bombings. Some came through unscathed. Some, like Fred, Shelagh, Sam, and thousands more were changed … they now ate flesh—human flesh—so they were truly zombies. They had kept the power of speech and nobody could tell them apart from the unchanged Ceti4 humans at all—unless one saw what they ate.

Others were affected worse. They had no real human characteristics at all. They could not talk, use tools, or do anything except chase food. As they lacked intelligence and ate any human flesh they could, these people, the dumb zombies, were at the bottom of the food chain here on Ceti4.

In between these two zombie classes were the dumb-now-smarter zombies who had been bitten by a smart zombie and regained their use of speech and could do simple tasks. Three classes of zombies now were on Ceti4, and from a simple first glance were almost all the same.

Fred answered his friend. "One of our team decided that he'd reach through the fence to get a better hold on the side of the replacement sheet of wire. He did that and then slowly cinched the new piece in place. The fact that his arm was then trapped seemed to matter not to him until he tried to walk away from the fence itself. He stepped away and then got yanked back—more than forty times by my count. He'd still be trying to get away from the fence if we hadn't simply cut him out of same," he said.

That got a laugh from them all, and they turned
to their left and went along the two-lane road back
toward the major part of the base. On their right lay
the barracks buildings, and Shelagh moved ahead
to point at the correct one for their team who peeled
off and went into the low single-floor barracks
building.

The rest of them went somewhat farther ahead,
and Sam stayed with Fred to report in to
administration on the day's work while his helper
and his dumb-now-smarter zombie team left the
road to go to their barracks. With more than two
hundred dumb-now-smarter zombies and teams,
the barracks were almost full.

On the left side of the base road lay enormous
buildings that had been used for various purposes
years ago. Now, they all sat and were mostly
unused, but the administration building just ahead
was where Fred and Sam were aiming. As they
mounted the stairs, another smart zombie named
Mark came down the steps and nodded to them as
he held the door open for them.

A large reception counter that was not used was
inside, and they made their way to a walkway to its
far side. Once past the counter, they moved to the
table that held some of their peers.

"Fred, how'd it go today?" one at the table asked,
and Fred relayed that they'd gotten more than three

whole sections done. Pretty good day, he figured, but he knew that it was just not enough for his questioner to accept.

"Three? Three whole sections? There's more than four thousand sections, Fred … three just isn't going to cut it," he said and frowned.

"Soon as you give me real workers I'll triple that, but until then …" he said, his voice trailing off.

"You and everyone else," the man said, and he looked up at Sam, who was shuffling on his feet.

"And you, Sam, how many did your team get done?"

"Two. But they were pretty bad—it was where those bandits cut their way in months ago to steal our trucks, and that took some doing too. We had to put half the team outside the fence to help so that meant that once the final section was done, we had to wait for them to walk like half a mile to the next big opening to get back into the base. Two … but a big two," he said.

The man at the table half-grinned at him. "So five between you both. Okay, fine … I'll make note of that. Same drill tomorrow, and if we can ask, could you all please try to get it amped up a bit … still thousands to go, eh?" he said, and his attention turned back to his tablet and the paperwork of being an administrator on the base.

Fred marched down the stairs still a bit upset

with how his three sections had been made so light of, and Sam caught up with him after a bit.

"Fred, don't worry. We're doing fine—and if you really think about it, it's like I've always been saying. This is all futile. No one will come in through the fence again—they'll just fly in with those machine gun dirigibles like last time. I still think that if we moved every single truck out of the Motor Pool and put them down say in the center of town, the base would stop being such a magnet," he said, and that got, as always, a nod from Fred.

"As you know, we did hide four of them in Walkerville at the arena, but that's just four trucks. Not the hundred in the Motor Pool building."

Someone wanted the base trucks. There were still more than a hundred in the Motor Pool building. And they'd come for them twice now. Once, through the fence, and they'd taken six, and once by that floating battleship and that had taken two more.

Move the trucks and lose their target status, he too had argued, but that had fallen on deaf ears at the administrative level.

He sighed. *Clean up, then dinner, then rest and chat a bit, and then bed … then more fence mending tomorrow …*

CHAPTER SIX

In her beautiful quarters in the dark tower, Jennifer sat at a small table against the big window and stared out at the lands around the castle. Since the tower was so high and no arrows could ever reach this level, this room had a true window. The large window gave her a spectacular view of the countryside. Below her, she knew well already, the windows in the castle were all of the tall, very narrow type—loopholes, they called them. Perfect for defense but not so much for viewing the countryside.

Beside her, but off to one side, was her beautiful four-poster bed. It was so big, she knew it would have slept ten. *Not*, she giggled for a second, *that she had ten people who she'd allow to sleep with her, but her sister Jessica would find it just as big as she did*, she thought.

Over on the far curved wall of the tower, there was a set of small tables and a big well-lit mirror with a counter before it that she'd been told was where she'd make herself look beautiful each day. As she had three banshee helpers—maids, Gisele had called them—to help her, she mostly sat on that stool in front of the mirror while others did her hair and her makeup and pinned on jewelry that she'd never seen before. There was a large, beautiful emerald broach, and she wondered what it might have cost. They always made her wear a necklace, and one of the maids always gave her a choice and asked pearls or gems. The maid who usually looked after her hair always placed something on her blonde locks. Some days, a headband, made from shells that gleamed in the light, was placed in her hair. Other days, it was clip that gathered up a loop of hair and gave her what she thought was a jaunty look.

No matter. I look as I always look, she thought, *but this sorceress lifestyle is so extravagant, and I haven't as yet even tasted it all.*

Out the window, the sun was lighting up some of the far ridges that glistened in the countryside. Jennifer wished she could go outside alone instead of remaining inside the castle, but Gisele and other banshees were always with her.

Part of her sorceress training involved tutoring sessions to learn the history of Castle Magic. Her tutor had told her that Castle Magic had been built hundreds of years ago to provide a safe haven for the king of this region. Built on rocky crags, it at one time held almost ten thousand inhabitants, but now the numbers were just a tenth of that. The sheer walls of the formidable structure climbed up almost two hundred feet before the ramparts. It was said that as recently as two hundred years ago, it had been under attack by the army from the north from Patch Bridge, a city she'd never heard of, and the castle had remained undefeated. Her tutor, a girl of about her own age, was nice, but she seemed to be more interested in learning about her and her way of life than in passing along history. Once, when she'd asked about the previous sorceress, she'd gotten such a strange look from Heidi, she'd had to ask again a second time. Heidi had nodded and changed the subject back to the castle and how thick it's walls were, but Jennifer asked a third time too.

Heidi, she remembered, had put a hand on her forearm and had squeezed it tightly. "No sense in trying to compare you to last year's sorceress—or any of them," she said, and she pointed instead down at the tome in front of her. "They come and they go," she said, and the lessons went on.

145

Jennifer looked out the window and stared across the rocky valley that the castle lay in. Green hills and a few farms were off in the distance. From here, she could see that the castle was well fortified and well supported too. She knew from her lessons that the rule here was that two years of food rations were always stored within the castle sub-basement areas. She had asked if she could see those stores, and Heidi had shot that idea down.

"No one wants to see row after row of hanging meat and bagged corn," she'd said, and she'd once again moved on with sharing information about the castle.

Jennifer didn't enjoy lesson after lesson of castle history, but she knew *that to be a valued member of any community, one should know as much as was possible about it—that had made sense back in her village those months ago, and it made sense now.*

She wondered how Jessica was and if the Forest Empire was still keeping her as a slave. Being a twin did make her feel different in all things, and her twin had always been at her side. Now, separated by hundreds of miles at least, she had no real feelings of Jessica being in trouble as had happened in the past.

She had felt some kind of an odd twin-based feeling just a few weeks ago in Lindos, though, like Jessica was close, but it had faded as soon as her new masters from Castle Magic had led her away from the slave block after buying her.

But now, those weeks gone by, she wasn't sure she had felt that at all.

Maybe just wishful thinking, she thought as she sipped from the water she'd been given by Heidi who'd left just an hour ago or so, lessons over for the day.

Maybe it was a part of just being a twin.

She didn't know any other twins to ask them how they felt, but she would if that chance ever presented itself.

She gazed out as far as she could see to the horizon in the east and wondered what life as the sorceress at Castle Magic would be like. She wondered how she would fit in with this new community and how she would become a part of it too.

#####

"A-one-one, confirming, in position now. Please chime in with your own status," the Regime marine colonel said. His voice was in monotone over the short-range walkie-talkies.

A platoon of marines sat behind him in the rear of the truck. Six trucks were on this mission to re-take the Walkerville Army Base, and each held a platoon of marines..

It had taken almost a day and a half for the company of marines to work their way from Arlington to Walkerville, using smaller regional roads only. Three times, they'd come on to groups of zombies—and they'd taken the time to finish them all off, to try to prevent any kind of forewarning to the smart zombies who held the base. Twice, they'd recovered radio devices, but one radio was broken, and the other had a dead battery. So, as the bird colonel hoped, Walkerville had no idea they were on their doorstep.

Two of the trucks had worked their way down the main street; they were the big army personnel carriers, and their job was to clear the street of any and all wrecks to provide—should it be needed—an escape route.

Colonel Solomon smiled. "We won't need any such route—it's 150 marines against some zombies—how hard can this be?" he said to himself.

A quick grimace reminded him that he'd had the exact same thought in other campaigns before, and he had been the one who'd had to make all those condolence calls to the families of soldiers he'd lost before.

No sense in feeling superior. Surprise is on our side, as is better arms and training and marines who can think on their feet.

But zombies were still feared—and the bitten

zombies, those zombies who'd been taken over by the smart variety, were generally an unknown. It was said they could bear arms and talk, and they just might be able to fight too.

He listened to all of the logins from the other five trucks and snapped on the soft red back-light on his tablet. Around him on the map, six red dots now surrounded the base.

Two were at the rear, facing the frost-wire fence that protected the drill field and then led to the main base road. One was on the west side, facing the twenty or so barracks buildings with only a row of hedges and then a low six-foot fence to mount. One truck was on the east side behind the huge Motor Pool building and the collateral support maintenance sheds that were lined up behind the same tall frost-wire fence. And the final two trucks, one of which he sat in, were on the road just a few hundred feet down the road that led to the base. These trucks were hidden in the dark shadows below the big elm trees that lined that street.

"All six in place—time to launch," he said to himself.

"Roger, five minutes to go time—from my mark," he said as he turned the tablet off and stowed it under his seat. "And … mark!" he said.

Each of the four trucks on the sides of the army base had a door open, and six men got out of the rear, each carrying a set of twenty-four-inch bolt cutters. Each took a section, reached as high as they could, and began to cut down the fence quickly making sure they cut each diamond equally. Eventually, the wires that held the fencing in its stretched position were on the ground. They cut that too, and the section they'd cut now sagged.

They got back into their respective trucks, which then started up. On each, the platoon lieutenant in the rear with his men said, "Night vision goggles on and get used to the few lights on the base," and they then waited for their countdown to end.

Up on the street that led to the base, the two trucks under the elms started up, lights fully blazing, and surged back onto the street. The lead truck with the colonel led the way the few hundred yards to where the road into the base met the street, and his truck turned almost on two wheels as the driver booted the truck with full acceleration. This truck had a large solid metal grate in front of the bumper that protected the windshield and the drive cab, and as the truck smashed into the closed frost-wire fence, it held and the truck roared through.

Shots rang out as the truck sped the few hundred feet down the main army base road and past the Motor Pool buildings to its right. It came to a rest at the first of the barracks buildings on its left. From the rear poured its platoon, and they were dispersing toward the barracks buildings ahead, running cautiously.

The second truck had followed the first one through the now smashed open security fence and stopped to block the only way into the base. Its platoon spilled out, and some went to the guard shack to deal with the zombies who'd opened fire already. Others ran back down the base road toward the Motor Pool building. Two of that platoon took up sniper positions, looking up at the roof of the Motor Pool, while the rest got to the door to hide among the pallets that were still stacked up nearby and take on a defensive position.

Ahead in the distance, the lights of the trucks that were off the base suddenly turned on, and the trucks smashed through the newly cut frost-wire fencing to move up the base road to take a position at the end of the rows of barracks. Out of their rears, their platoons surged toward the barracks to begin to locate the enemy and take them out.

On both sides of the base, the last two trucks smashed through their own fences and took up positions around the Motor Pool and the administration building as well, and their platoons engaged with zombies.

"Lieutenant," Colonel Solomon said to the closest platoon leader, "get going on those barracks. Send out an advance squad with ordnance. I want every single one of these barracks on fire in five minutes," he said.

The lieutenant shouted, "Aye, Sir," as he turned to command his platoon who he sent off to do the colonel's bidding, and in less than five minutes, all of the barracks buildings were aflame.

Outside each, a brace of three marines stood, mowing down every single body that left the now burning buildings. Some zombies realized the buildings were on fire, and they'd broken out through side windows. Yet the marines found them and shot them. Two of the barracks had returned fire, and a couple of medics were now working on downed marines.

At the back of the Motor Pool building, some zombies lay behind the building where they'd fallen after taking fire as they'd tried to escape. The truck covering that spot had seen the group of zombies crawling around the corner of the Motor Pool building and had sprayed them down.

At the administration building, there appeared to have been some zombies within, and they'd been cut down quickly. Smart zombies, the colonel thought, would be the only ones in any administration building in his world, and he made a note to check on any intel he could find there later.

He stood up on the passenger side bumper of his

truck, and from what he could see, the attack had been a success. Mop-up would occur once the gunfire ended, and he'd get the firefight stats then. But so far, so good.

Good enough to report in, he felt.

He dropped off the bumper, and one of their marine snipers ahead fired. The sound of their weapon was one he enjoyed, and it barked three times, as he walked over to the marine who was leaning on a young sapling for support.

"Three shots to get one zombie, Carruthers?" he said and grinned at the sniper.

"Sir, three shots for two zombies—one of them popped up and down twice, so I wanted to make sure, Sir," he said and ,grinned back at his colonel.

"Carry on, lad," the colonel said as he traced his path back to the cab of his truck.

As he did, his walkie-talkie began to chime, and he took calls from all of his lieutenants in each of the five other trucks.

All in all, seven marines had been hit—only one seriously and he was in good hands with the medics. While they were still sifting through the barracks, which were still smoking and in some cases, still aflame, they took a count of the dead, and the number of dead zombies climbed to more than a hundred. There were also at least twenty smart zombies also dead. The administration building had five more, it seemed, and the roof of the Motor Pool had three more.

All enemy resistance is now over was the general feeling of his officers, and the mop-up continued.

He nodded to himself, fished his tablet out from under his seat, and jammed him thumb against the pad to wake it up. Moments later, he was talking live to the Regime back in Arlington. He reported the attack on the army base as successful, gave his firefight stats, and asked for permission to re-fortify the base as per the second part of his mission.

The Regime congratulated him on his and his men's success, gave him the go-ahead to get the base back into a secure shape, and told him to expect new soldiers, supplies, and fortifications once the trucks were sent back and then out to him again.

He nodded, but they couldn't see that, he knew, so he said, "Aye, HQ. Will send the trucks back at first light, over and out," and he sat back to look out over the base.

Fires still burned off to his left as the barracks were still smoldering. He ordered the groups of marines who were off to his far left and far right to unload their trucks of all supplies. Their next job was to fix the fences where they'd all smashed through just an hour ago.

He'd ordered the lieutenant on his truck to get

the tents setup for his company, and he'd also
sought out the quartermaster to get some food
going via MREs and find the base latrines and let
the men know.

Being in charge of a firefight was one thing, but
running an army base was another. He grinned at
his wit and went on a grand tour of the base, his
private having found a Jeep that worked in the
Motor Pool building.

Sitting in the open vehicle, he was driven first to
the barracks to see what remained. Nothing that
could be used for his men, he quickly saw, and
while that was a shame, the bodies of zombies laid
out beside them reminded him that it was so much
easier to do it this way by forcing them out with fire
than going building by building for hand-to-hand
combat.

"Lieutenant," he called out.

A marine ahead of him turned back. "Sir?" he
asked.

"Lieutenant, get over to the Motor Pool and see if
you can find a bulldozer or something like it. I want
a mass grave dug—you decide where, but one big
enough to hold all these zombie bodies. Soon as the
wind comes up tomorrow, the smell of their flesh
will attract more, and we don't need that kind of
ongoing enemy attention right now. STAT,
Lieutenant, I want those bodies all buried by

dawn," he said, and he motioned for the private to drive on.

As they went back across the grass toward the main road, he pointed to his left, and the private went down the road away from the center of the base. After a few hundred yards, the road curled to the right, around what looked like some kind of distribution building, and then again to the right to come up between the big Motor Pool building to his right and the support and maintenance buildings to his right. As they got closer, four shapes crossed the road running from the right to the left side and toward the fence.

"Gun her, private," he said and he reached for his .45 Colt that he carried on his hip. Whoever that had been, they weren't dressed like his marines, which meant they were the enemy, and as the Jeep squealed to a stop at the narrow alley between two of the outbuildings, he jumped out of the seat and tore down the alley.

Ahead of him was mostly darkness, but the lighter-colored siding on the walls of the building gave him some light. At the end of the building, he stopped and quickly ducked down to stick his head out much lower than anyone would expect.

There was nothing to his right, and as he leaned against the building on his left and his eyes darted to his left, he saw them.

156

Two figures were about three-quarters over the fence, climbing it quickly, and on the other side, two more were urging them on.

He rose and with careful aim, he put a slug into the uppermost climber, who was straddling the top and leaning over to offer a hand to the last of them, and he fell backward with a shout.

He aimed at the second climber who had frozen in its climb, and he shot that one too. He looked through the fence to see that the two that had already gotten over were now running away full tilt. He aimed slowly and pulled the trigger, but the sparks his bullet made as it ricocheted off the fence meant he'd missed. And now they were gone.

He swore. There was no chance to catch them now—the fence protected them as much as it'd been made to protect the base. He went over to the two bodies and turned them over with a shoe.

One was a male zombie, smart zombie too, he noted that was dead. That was the one who'd been straddling the top of the fence. The other was a female smart zombie, who appeared to not be doing so well. She was choking, and it appeared his bullet had hit her in the lungs.

A shot rang out. The private stepped forward and said, "Got her for you, Sir," and he put his pistol back into his holster at his side.

The colonel was not surprised, but he tried to

never miss a chance to educate his men either. "Yes, Private, thank you. But I'd have waited to ask her some questions—intel gathering is very important out in the field, Private. Then when I knew I'd gotten all I could, I'd have shot her. Maybe try to remember that for next time?" he asked, and the private nodded so much the colonel thought he'd shake off his ears.

They made their way back to the Jeep and then back over to the administration building. Meeting some of his lieutenants, he set up base HQ there, and the night went on toward the dawn.

As the group passed across the bridge, Javor was most interested in seeing the *Drake* and how she looked as one came up on her from the streets. The bridge that passed over the river still had the same hulks of the cars and a truck on same, and there was nothing really new to see at that level. He remembered how Bruce had helped clear the bridge those months ago—well, Jimmy had actually done the luring of the dumb zombies to get their attention, and Bruce had shot four of them to create the diversion that had cleared the bridge.

"Jimmy," he said to himself, "had been one hell of a chef here on Bones." His death that night in the storm had been a real loss to them, and he had to shake off that feeling as they tromped over the bridge.

"Can't really even see her anymore," Sue said as they moved off the bridge onto the street that ran parallel with the river and the ridge line well above. There, the *Drake* lay but she was now covered in undergrowth from below, and the trees around her shrouded her in dappled sunlight too. Lying where she was, the *Drake* had been slowly hidden by the growth of the forest around her, and one could see that in a month or two more, she'd be invisible from above.

Bixby barked and Javor scratched his ear and nodded to the dog and the rest of them too. "That's a good thing," he replied to Sue as they moved over the road, up the curb, through the low hedge, and then into the thick copse to slowly begin to climb up to the ship. As Vera was not as agile as some, Javor held the pace to a slow climb, and it took almost a half hour to climb the few hundred yards of little hillocks, bumps, and dips on the shoulders of the ridge. Often they had to be careful as their feet searched for purchase on the rocky outcrops, but all in all, the six of them reached the ship with no real hardship.

"Not a single zombie, smart or dumb," Wayne said as he turned to keep watch behind them and below them back down across the river into

Maxwell.

Jon had chosen to come along as he'd never been on a spaceship, and he looked ahead. "So, she's way the hell up in the trees—how do we get up there?" he asked as he leaned on a sapling and looked up.

It was twenty or so feet to the bottom of the hull, and Javor knowing the answer said, "We just ask for the ship to bend down, Jon."

He moved to stand at the front of the group and said clearly and loudly, "AI—this is Javor Novak. Please acknowledge and do a voice-print authorization—six, thirteen, twenty-two forty-nine."

There was no answer from the *Drake*'s AI, but Javor knew it was computing his voice against the database voiceprint it held in the ship's archives.

A full minute later, the AI spoke back to him. "Confirmed, Javor. Please tell me the color of your first flyer," it asked.

Javor was the only one who could answer the confirmation question. His answer would confirm that he stood at the ship's front edge. "Orange."

The single word he said was met first with silence and then a triple chime sounded. The front airlock door slid open, and down came the boarding ramp.

"Correct, Javor. Orange it was … welcome back. You have been gone 189 days—you will need to reset your confirmation question and also your entry levels as well," the *Drake* AI said, and the slowly lowering ramp touched the ground just in front of him.

He grinned to them all and said, "Come on aboard," and he hustled up the ramp, but Bixby beat him into the ship.

Once inside, Jon whistled and grinned almost at the same time. "Wow, spaceman—you have a great ride here," he said as he dropped into the pilot's seat on the left side of the big ship's dashboard.

Javor said to the AI, "Please display the view ahead, sidebar with last diagnostics, and I'd also like a full report on stores—especially on the batteries. Life, amp levels, juice runway burn—you know the drill, AI. Soon as it's done, chime and display."

The whole front end of the huge cockpit came alive as the town of Maxwell was now being displayed. On the left side of the large live screen, a sidebar showed some settings and archived materials that made little sense to most on the bridge, but Javor did take the time to read same as he dropped his backpack and his shotgun onto the floor.

"Made promises to you all—follow me for the showers, clothing, and galley tour," he said.

In twenty minutes, he was back on the bridge but alone. Vera and Sue had co-opted the showers first after finding some clothing that would fit from the crew's cabins. Jon, Wayne, and Bruce were investigating the galley and the freezer areas to come up with something to eat. They were next in the showers, and he'd join them then.

Now, he sat in the co-pilot's seat and stared up at the sidebar. He looked to the battery life area first and realized after some quick figuring that the *Drake* was now within two months of being out of power totally. Nuclear reactor had been shut down those six months ago, and battery power had kept the ship alive but really hibernating. Battery life was down to eleven percent—he'd need to run the reactor for at least a day, he knew, to gain back that full one hundred percent re-charge.

"AI, bring the reactor back online." he said. "Authorizations Nancy, thirty-three, Y, U, eight."

Nancy had been the *Drake*'s captain and her pilot —so he mentally gave a little dip of his head to her. She'd died in the Boathi attack those months ago as had the whole crew, except for him.

Around him, there was a sense of things happening within the ship. There was no noise of the reactor as the rods came out of their storage bins and were slowly being re-inserted into the pile, but he thought—and he realized he was wrong, of course—that the whole view-screen brightened just a bit. The lights on the bridge seemed a bit yellower, but he knew he was wrong. AI controlled the reactor so minutely that there was supposed to be no noticeable change, yet he still thought he could tell.

He spent the next ten minutes reading the scrolling text that read that the reactor was back online; in twenty-one hours, the *Drake* would once again be fully charged. He wondered about its flight-worthiness once again.

He also realized he'd missed a chance earlier when he'd taken supplies from the *Drake* those long months ago. This time, he saw a small icon—grayed out now—that looked like a megaphone on the view-screen sidebar. It was the *Drake*'s AI notification ability—if he told the AI to notify him personally on issues that he could list for AI to monitor, he would get a notice if he took a monitor device with him. Small, only an inch or so square, it could be put in a pocket or on his belt. He thought about that for a moment and then nodded to himself.

"AI, please turn on notifications. I want you to notify me if you get any kind of Boathi presence found STAT. STAT, mind you, AI," he said, "and I mean anything and everything you find, AI. Understood?" he asked.

AI chimed three times, indicating a positive response. He leaned over the dashboard to reach above same and pop open the tray above the dash. He looked inside and took out one of the fully charged small units. He clicked it onto his belt and turned it on at the same time.

Okay, if the Boathi show up, I'd know soonest.

That one is done. Can't believe I'd missed that chance months ago, but I'm smarter now, maybe, he thought and sighed.

"AI, please run a complete and full set of diagnostics. I want to know if I took the *Drake* up— powered flight—again, what might happen. Would she fly okay? For how long? Are there any hurdles that I should know about before such an attempt? Pretend that I'm so new to being a pilot that nothing—nada—should be skipped over. I want that report in less than a day too, AI. Get going …" he said, and the AI chimed once to signify it was working.

He smiled and trooped out of the bridge, past the galley where Wayne shouted that tonight they'd be having old world spaghetti and meatballs and garlic bread—and they'd even found some wine too. He nodded and kept going, through the crew's quarters and down the hallway there to the door to the armory.

"AI—six, thirteen, twenty-two forty-nine, please," he said, and the door to the large room opened up silently.

Inside, he ignored the right-hand wall with its bows and arrows and swords and the left-hand wall with the ordnance, grenades, and mortars. Instead he marched straight ahead and grinned as he pulled out a deep drawer to free a brand new combat shotgun from its holder.

He smiled. He hefted it and looked it over. He broke down the magazine and confirmed that all was well and then reached back into the drawer for three of those forty-shell magazines. He snapped one into place, scooped up the other two, and then went back to the bridge. Halfway there, he realized he'd not checked his Colt ammunition, and when went back to the armory to get a few more clips, he found Bruce there looking around.

"One you want," he said as he returned the favor, "is in the third drawer from the left, bottom row," he said, grabbed the clips for his Colt, and left the armory.

He was pleased to see Bruce appear on the bridge ten minutes later with a brand new sniper rifle in his hands.

Bruce grinned. "Much obliged, Javor. Loved that gun—too bad those Forest Empire goons took it," he said.

"Not that it'll do them much good in a city that has a nuke crater instead of a downtown," Javor replied, and that got them both to laughing.

As Vera and Sue, their hair wet but looking much refreshed, entered the bridge, Sue spoke up first.

"New weapons always get smiles—but why the laugh?" she inquired, and Bruce explained, and they all had a good laugh.

"Head is free," Vera added as she toweled her hair dry.

"Thanks—our turn then," Javor said as he led Bruce back to the crew quarters and then off to port.

Wayne was already in one of the shower stalls, under the spray, and he was singing some kind of ditty and off tune to boot, Javor thought, and soon all were showered, dressed again, and in the galley.

As Sue dished out the sauce, Wayne placed three meatballs on top and the dinner was on.

While he'd really not liked being a marine those twenty years ago, Javor knew that it was times like this—normal life—that made his old squad bond and become a whole. That's how he felt now, and he wished that Toby and Jessica had joined them instead of staying behind to run checks on the floater. Patrollers Kyle and Rick had offered to help, and they were stocking up Zoe's freezers with some food stuffs from the cadre's freezers in the courthouse.

Vera twirled her fork into her spoon like a pro and said between bites, "So, how long 'til the *Drake* is fully re-charged. And why, if you don't mind me asking, do you bother to take the reactor offline anyways?"

Her question was apropos, Javor thought, and the answer came from his Human Empire Explorer training. "Boathi use some kind of their superior technology to find our ships. We don't really know how that works—but I can tell you that after years of testing—if the reactor on a ship is offline, they go right on by. Seems that our reactors have some kind of a signature that they can scan for, so that's why I took the *Drake* offline."

She nodded. "Course, that's if they get close maybe? Or do they use a satellite system to find a human ship? Or …?"

He shrugged. "That I don't know—the Empire might—but in our training, all we were taught was to deactivate the reactor to be invisible to their scans. In less than twenty hours, our batteries will be back up to par, and I'll take the reactor offline again, so we'll be sleeping here tonight," he said.

"Dibs on that bunk with the pictures of all those beautiful vid stars," Wayne said and grinned at him.

Smiling, they finished their dinner, and while Bixby looked like he wanted to go out, Javor hit the hay and let Jon take care of that duty After showing him how to seal the ship back up as night was falling on Maxwell.

#####

The sub-alternate's hate of something askew was the cause of his current plight. The grid pattern was not being used, and the flashing pink lines on the huge view-screen sideboard reminded him of that repeatedly. His task, as it had been now for six days since the captain had issued the ten-day window, was to look for the lights of cities, study them with a scan, and then move on. The southern continent had been finished, and they'd moved on to the larger northern continent just two days ago.

As the terminator slowly moved across the continent, his job was to position the *Sophon* in the dark to look for lights that came up over the horizon. When a center big enough—a real judgment call, he knew—came along, he dropped down to twenty thousand feet to do proper scans and record same. If anything was odd or different or stuck out, he'd drop down even closer for a visual with the very large resolution *Sophon* telescopes and record same to the *Sophon*'s database archive too.

That hadn't happened, but something was sticking out in his reptile brain, as he scratched the nape of his scaly neck. With no superior officer on the bridge at this time of night, he could scratch away any itches that occurred.

Just a night ago, when the *Sophon* had been on high cruise at ten miles up, something had chimed. It was so unusual, he'd immediately slowed the ship, spun her to drop down to two miles up, and re-scanned that same stretch in the foothills near a mountain range. A quick scan of metallic ores showed no beryl deposits though which again worried him.

At this much lower level, anything that meant the *Sophon* had detected nuclear activity should have been easy to find and to see.

Nothing. No nuclear power of any kind, so no human spaceship either.

Yet something had made the high pass over the area chime—and he'd asked for a full report on that scan and those chimes at the end of yesterday's shift. He'd thought of notifying the captain then too, but he had decided that this was not such a good idea. To have the captain think one thing and then have it just be some kind of an equipment malfunction would surely see his eggs destroyed.

He fingered his console and looked for the report, and seeing same, he gained access at his station. He read it quickly. He paused twice to re-read the same passage, ensured that the GPS co-ordinates were recorded for same, and then closed the report.

It said nothing.

No human ship with a nuclear reactor had been found. In fact, it was not about any kind of nuclear materials at all. The *Sophon* had simply bumped into a cloud of beryllium oxide, which was always something to chime about. While the *Sophon* was not on an exploratory mission looking for ore, the location of that cloud was noted and would be in the Boathi archives forever.

Still, it bothered him somewhat, and he had no idea why.

#####

As Zoe floated along, Toby was busy at the stick, and Javor thought that just a bit odd.

"Toby, something wrong?" he asked as the floater moved along about five thousand feet up and above the mountains below them.

This range ran from the northeast to the southwest and was at least a hundred miles wide. This range had big, twisted, and folded mountains with enormous valleys covered with snow and ice. Not a single animal had been seen since they'd left Maxwell, just a couple of hours ago. Maxwell lay just about due east of Castle Magic, so the trip over the range was just about a straight line, due west.

"The mountains are always tricky," Toby said as he once again twisted the stick to port, and the floater's nose slowly moved to the left and then back on course. "It's the currents and eddies up here, where the westerly winds find a way below, there's often up-swellings of huge air movements. Makes Zoe react and we need to watch them carefully," he said as he then moved the stick to starboard.

Below, the group could see the arêtes of this young mountain range were knife-like and sharp with glacial carving done long ago. There were the occasional pyramidal shapes too, where there had been more than a couple of those eroding glaciers over eons. The cirques beneath were snow covered and deep but untracked. No human had probably ever been on the lands below nor would they, Javor thought, unless Zoe decided to go down. He grinned at that. No way.

Toby piloted the floater with skill, and it moved in a slightly snaky fashion toward the horizon, where Castle Magic lay. They were still hours away, but as they moved toward same, the scenery below changed yet remained the same. White snow, ice sheets, and rough rock mountains. Nothing lived below and wouldn't be able to. Javor filed that away in his mental archive under the check box of lands that were not habitable.

After a quick lunch, which Wayne and Jon had rustled up from some of their supplies, and then cleanup too, Javor found himself sitting in the co-pilot's seat while Jessica, Zoe's normal co-pilot, was busy.

"Toby, tell me. Is there any real truth to these Castle Magic people actually having some kind of magic at their beck and call?" he asked.

Toby nodded. "Once a few years back, a small group of same came to the Forest Empire, to talk to the disciples—no idea what the topic was. But someone did ask—I had to fly them around on a tour of the city—if they had magic. They just looked at the disciple who'd asked and had said nothing. But later, I heard that same disciple talking to others, and he said that when they'd left, they'd just disappeared. One second they were there, then they were gone—into thin air. That'd be magic, in my world," he said.

Javor could tell by the tone of his voice that he believed it was magic. He smiled. "There might be many answers to why and how that might have happened. I have no idea, but I know that for sure," he said, and they both sat, thinking on that as a whole bank of the mountains below went by.

As the horizon was changing, Javor pointed it out and that got a nod from Toby.

"Yup, end of the mountain range coming up in about an hour—then the rolling hills and mesas and hillocks run another forty miles or so, eventually fading into the huge flatlands beyond. Castle Magic lies near the end of those rolling hills; it's mounted on a spire of rock that juts up and out of the valley around it. Very much a spot that could have been defended hundreds of years ago when armies would invade, I'd guess."

"And now," Javor asked, looking for any knowledge at all about this new society.

"Now, it's the home of this group of people that my old boss in OilCo used to call a cult—until the Forest Empire killed him and most of the leaders of the company. Cults. Many of them now like the Forest Empire are just one group of people who use myth or rumor or force to get their own way—and I suspect these guys are the same," he said.

He wiped his brow as he steered the stick first left and then left again as Zoe vibrated in the winds from below.

Javor nodded. He'd thought as much and realized that after the Boathi had bombed the planet, many of the cults had grown in the vacuum of real civilization, hence the reappearance of slavery and the force of the cults. Without an overall society and the trappings of same, anything could happen—and it had.

He shook his head and frowned. Many times before, he'd been saddened by what the Drake had found left in the wake of the Boathi incursion into the Human Empire worlds. He really didn't know what was worse—the bombed craters with just zombies and dead civilization or the rebuilding of same but with cults and slavery. No way to tell, he knew, but still it was something that only one group was responsible for—the Boathi.

He smiled. *One day … one day soon,* he knew, *he'd have the chance to hurt them … and hurt them badly if he could.*

Toby bent the stick to port and reached over to slow the throttles on Zoe's motors. "That's Castle Magic ahead," he said.

A castle, yes, Javor thought, *but what a castle it is!*

Various turrets, towers, and domed structures that all were intertwined with streets and the very walls of the castle itself loomed in the distance. The castle was many shades of brown with golden-colored roofs. It looked big enough to hold a few thousand people, he thought, but then as Zoe moved slowly to port, he could see all the extra space on the far side.

It had been built on what would be called a rock tower—weathered by the sea and air over eons.

Around it, the valley held many, many farms. Against the far edge, there appeared to be some kind of a strip mine that lay right up beside the start of the mountains there. From where Zoe sat, it was ten miles away at least, but even at that distance, one could see the cloud of dust that such a facility would create.

The castle sat on that rock tower, one of the three that jutted up from the valley. Up top, the capstone —the top of the tower rock itself—was harder than what was beside and partially below the tower, so it had maintained the height of almost a hundred yards or so. The width of the tower was at least three hundred yards wide, so the tower was quite formidable, standing as it did beside a couple of other rock towers in the valley of the foothills. Those other towers were linked to the castle with walkways that hung like all suspended bridges hung and were most likely very tricky to walk on, Javor thought. It would be even trickier to try to run a force of men down same as a simple cut of a sword would cut the bridge at either end, and that'd mean a fall of those hundred yards to the ground well below.

From where Zoe came, over the mountains and then dropping down to circle the castle, they realized that such a momentous arrival might be seen as being aggressive, so Toby was under orders from Sue to drop her quickly on the field below the castle, which he was in the process of doing.

As Zoe got lower and lower, a group of some kind of men—only about ten or so, Javor thought— were making good time out of the huge drawbridge at the castle's front end, across the moat which was really a river that ran around the castle's rock tower and then across a wide gravel road toward the floater. They were not running but marched in stride and soon were positioned between the floater and the castle. Around them, the road that had held occasional pedestrians and farmers' carts was empty; in fact, it was totally quiet and still.

Sue preceded them all down the level to the boarding area, and as the walkway dropped down, Toby yelled, "All docked," and she nodded as she went down the ramp to the grass below, just in front of the group that met their advance.

She walked out with Vera at one side and Jon on the other. Behind her, Javor, Wayne, and Bruce lined up and completed the agreed-upon landing party. Each was armed with their long guns, but all were shouldered and presented no real threat. Each also had a sidearm, and Javor rested his palm on his Colt. Again, no threat but then none was really meant either.

One of the robed castle inhabitants stepped forward and smiled at them. "I am Gray Mage Gadsby. We welcome you and your fellow visitors to Castle Magic," he said and partially bowed or dipped his head. Javor couldn't tell which, but it was a good sign, he thought.

Sue smiled in return. "And I am Sue Fines—of

the Regime— the government of Ceti4 located in Arlington. We are pleased to be so welcomed," she said and then introduced the six who accompanied her.

The mage nodded to each, said welcome five more times, and introduced the man to his left. "And this is Banshee Gaspar—my personal banshee —and the rest of these castle men are reapers—our helpers. As I said, we welcome you to our castle— but a small note please for you to learn right away? It is our custom that you learn at the first opportunity that we mages are protected with the spell of invulnerability—at least that's what it's called by our citizens," he said as he stepped forward from the rest of his group.

"I see that you carry arms—both of the long kind and the ones you put on your belts too. Could I ask please that one of you—all of you, if you'd like— would attempt to shoot me, please?" he said with a dry tone.

Sue half-stepped back. "Mage Gadsby, it is not our intent to hurt anyone—ever, so this is—"

He waved her off and said, "Your arms are not going to hurt us—please, would someone please try to shoot me—the spell will not allow me to be injured at all."

Before anyone else could even move, Bruce half-turned, the sniper rifle falling into his hands, and he clicked the safety off, chambered a shell, and fired directly at the mage in less than a second.

The report of the firing was loud. But the mage stood and then smiled and nodded to Sue and Bruce too.

"As I said—and as you've all just learned—we are invulnerable. Our magic protects us, so please while we do not mind you bearing arms into the castle, we can assure you that they do not work on us—mages and above. Oh, you can kill a farmer or a banshee, that is true, and such an event will cause the shooter to give up their lives, but that's all negative. On the positive side, we always welcome new visitors to Castle Magic. Would you like to come with me for a tour? We have already started plans on a welcome dinner for tonight when you will meet the warlock—our leader—and you will also have some time for a rest too after your voyage on that wonderful floating airship too."

CHAPTER SEVEN

On the *Drake*, it was quiet, as it was supposed to be, after everything had been shut down and the reactor had been taken offline. The recent visit by the last crew member, Javor, had been over now for almost a week. The hibernation had begun, and it would continue.

AI came online with five chimes, and lights blinked on the dash as AI came out of hibernation. Fully awake and now in charge of the ship, the AI had a job to do, and it first double-checked its telltales.

The *Drake* scanned the atmosphere around it all day long, among thirty other scans that it ran on a daily or hourly basis. The latest atmosphere scan had happened all of seven minutes ago.

Atmosphere had been taken in by an array on the

top of the ship. It had undergone standard gas chromatography analysis, and it had found an anomaly—it found a high concentration of beryllium oxide. This was so much of an anomaly that the fact it'd been found kicked the AI into wake-up mode.

AI checked the sample. It checked again and confirmed that beryllium oxide had been found. The sample said that the concentration was well above 0.025 mg/m3—it was lethal should it be inhaled by humans at almost double that strength.

The toxicity of the cloud of gas that the prevailing westerly winds had brought did not concern the AI, but what that meant—according to the Human Empire database which the AI had checked with— triggered additional procedures from AI.

Beryllium as an ore was used for many things but never for any item found on a Human Empire spaceship. It was used only on Boathi sphere ships where plates or foils of beryllium were usually used as pushers for the implosion of plutonium-239. When it was properly taken care of, the reactor it was a part of ran fine, but as it began to break down, oxides formed, and that could be dangerous to any and all who might breathe in the deteriorating plates.

The fact that AI had detected a cloud of beryllium could mean there was a Boathi sphere ship in some degree of being or becoming a hazard. Could was the active word as the AI and its deciding algorithm was more positive than negative, and the AI knew as a result of that judgment, it had to notify all on the notifications list of this possible Boathi presence.

AI looked up the notifications queue and found that it was supposed to send through the notice of this occurrence to the last remaining crew member, Javor, and that he'd requested the information STAT.

It turned on its device notification app, composed the message, and then sent it STAT to the crew member. Javor would receive it in seconds. There was a small chance—twenty-one percent the algorithm said—of the Boathi now being on Ceti4.

That information was sent with the estimate of where the cloud had originated and in what direction, and that was done using an icon on a map of the mountain range where it was estimated the winds had come from, the direction of the winds, and the time line too. The icon sat on the far western edge of the mountain range in the neighborhood of an area that was named Castle Magic.

All that went out to the final crew member in less than a second. AI archived the data and sent a further notification to the Human Empire HQ—but that, of course, just sat in the queue as there was no working satellite network above to send it out at FTL.

AI shut down and the *Drake* grew dark once more. Its job done, AI went back into hibernation until something else happened.

Colonel Solomon smiled. "This town is like all the other towns I've been in throughout the last few years," he said to himself as he rode into Walkerville from the army base they'd taken over just last night. It was a quiet ride, and his driver took extra care to stop every few hundred yards to get the good to go message from the scouts up ahead on foot. They were in an army personnel carrier with an armed squad in the back—he'd been loath to enter town in a truck that advertised snacks on the side.

Call it marine pride, he thought, and he grinned.

Three scouts had been sent out ahead, solid marine scouts all hooked up via walkie-talkies with the colonel's truck to let them know what was found. Or what wasn't found.

Moving out of the base, they turned to their right and down the empty street toward town. A single white line down the center of the road appeared, and they followed the line.

Ahead about two hundred yards, sidewalks started again, and they stopped and waited for the first scouting reports which were positive—no enemy found so far—and his driver powered up once again.

Empty lots appeared and overgrown grass strips lined the cracked and disheveled streetscape. One of the few remaining houses had been boarded up. Sheets of plywood covered all the doors and windows, and the front door had an iron gate in front of it. The colonel almost stopped to check it out, but then he saw that the side of the house had been burned and was now showing its insides, charred floors and empty hallways all deserted.

They motored on, and in about a half mile more, they stopped waiting for the scouts' report. The report finally came, but it took longer than they'd wanted, and the colonel was no longer smiling.

Ahead, the wrecks of cars and trucks had been piled into a tall heap at the center of the road. Before that pile lay a crater, which was deep and full of what he thought was the wreckage of a building that had once stood there.

His driver, a gunnery sergeant named Kurt, offered up an explanation as they sat and waited. "Sir, the crater is where a power substation sat— took big watts from the Adair Dam and de-tuned them for local use—and the Boathi made sure it was gone, Sir," he said.

Solomon looked at it, and he knew his gunny was right. *The crater was more than twenty yards deep, filled with what looked like twisted and warped I-beams and metal trusses. Demolished porcelain insulators were in chips and flakes all over the walls of the crater. From what he could see, rainwater filled up the bottom of the crater, and its brown surface was like a chocolate mirror. For a moment,* he wondered *how deep it was, but then the scouts signed in.*

"Colonel, you're good to go to the four-way stop about a half mile past that crater," one of them said.

The gunny restarted the truck and they moved on. The road was now three lanes with the middle one, he suspected, used to turn off the road, and their truck was in that lane as they moved down the street.

On the sides, there were at first occasional retail stores, all closed and empty, and some had lost all their glass. In a couple of cases, the whole storefront was gone. He saw a cupcake place—at least that's what he thought the sign out front, though askew, offered up for sale. *Beside it was an auto parts store, and the fact it adjoined a cupcake store made him wonder about who had done the feasibility study on location placement, but that was for another time.*

The number of stores grew as the commercial district became more heavily populated as the truck moved into the area just off the core of the town. At a stop sign ahead, the gunny stopped the truck once again, and they sat in the intersection itself. Off to the right, about a mile or two away, they could see the interstate highway. They'd not yet used the interstate as they had driven from Arlington to Walkerville on regional roads only. Partly, he knew, because it was believed that regional roads were more secure, but also, he thought, so that the trip would show all of the tribes that the Regime had trucks—was powered by old technology, but that they'd brought it back to life.

Sort of true, he thought, *but then again, as long as the people who saw the trucks knew it was the Regime, that was what counted. The fact that the trucks that had been driven here to Walkerville all had their logo—the red arrow below the gold star—meant that anyone who knew the Regime saw their power.*

He smiled. *Power is as power does,* he thought.

There were four gas stations at this major intersection, each burned out and a shell of what they might have been like. Four different brands too, he noted. He did remember the Yellow Rose one—he'd worked at a station much like the one to his right when he'd been a summer student, filling tanks with gasoline and washing windows clean. Kitty-corner from it was the only other one he knew called BP—he had no idea what that stood for, but he had used it himself when he'd had a car before the Boathi had come to Ceti4. A station he'd not recognized with the name GasGo was off to his left. Lastly, there was a SuperTest station., He remembered he'd used them only once and his car had run like hell after the fill up. *Water in the gas,* he'd figured those many years ago, and today, he was happy that the station looked like it had gotten the worst of the bombing the Boathi had brought to Walkerville.

Still waiting for the next scout reports, he looked over top of the stations ahead and toward the downtown area, the core, as they called it. He wondered *just how much of it was left,* and after the check-in by the scouts that happened as he thought that, the truck moved on as gunny started her up, and they moved through the intersection itself.

Three more blocks and then a left turn onto the main street—Main Street it was called, quite accurately, here in Walkerville. Angle parking was on both sides of the street, and hulk after destroyed hulk of cars and pickups and even some motorcycles were all badly burned up.

Storefronts were all broken up, and some had been boarded up too. There was no sign of anyone, however, to his eyes.

"Sir—found some folks. Not a worry—families and seniors mostly, all over near the town park.

Appears to be a farmer's market that's open, Sir.
Do you wish us to engage or simply watch and
observe, Sir?"

Solomon considered and then radioed back to
them. "Let them be—we'll be there in like a minute
or so—we'll talk to them. Look all the way to the
end of town down Main Street, and then curl to the
east and come back to the four-way stop. Out," he
said.

He motioned to gunny to move off, and in less
than a minute, the large park that lay just off the
core area of town appeared on the right. There was
a large parking lot with a couple of abandoned cars
off to one side. Two baseball diamonds lay near the
center of the park and a couple of soccer pitches
were farther out. In the center of the park was a
brick building that probably used to house
washrooms and the like, but now was boarded up
completely.

The people were the focus of his gaze, once he
found them way down at the end of the parking lot.
There were a few rows of what looked like wagons
with some mules off to one side, grazing on the
grass that was so overgrown on the close baseball
field. As his truck slowly turned into the park and
made for the end of the parking area, he saw people
around those wagons. He tapped his gunny on the
shoulder and said, "Park her here, Gunny," and

the truck came to a stop.

He got out, banged the side of the passenger door twice, and then slowly made his way toward the group of people well ahead. Behind him, the squad in the rear was getting out and following along, all spread out and casing the site for any risk.

As he got to the knot of people at one side, Solomon stopped and smiled at them. He was in his marine fatigues, no long gun but a holstered Colt on his hip, and he held out his hand, palm toward them, and said, "Hi."

No one said anything from the closest group of people, but then a youngster of about ten stepped forward and said "Hi.".

That seemed to break the ice, and the girl's mother swooped forward to hug her girl and drag her back to the group.

He smiled. "Nice to meet you, young lady. My name is Solomon—Colonel Solomon—of the Regime. You might have heard of us, we're the last remaining government here on Ceti4, and while we are new to Walkerville, we're here to stay. So good to meet you—meet you all," he said, and he took a pace forward and stuck out his hand to shake the young girls hand.

Her dad, at least that's what he figured, stepped forward instead and shook his hand, and yes, the ice was broken. He shook everyone's hand, and there was more than a dozen people. He let them know he'd probably forget all their names, and that got a laugh.

"Not my name," the young girl said. "My name is Gladys, and you must remember me!" she said loudly and oh-so precociously.

He grinned at her. "Ah … Gladys. No, I'll never forget that name," he said, and he shook her hand last. He grinned again as he reached into his vest pocket and took out a fresh chocolate bar, which he'd gotten from the stores of snack foods they'd found in the base Motor Pool. and he handed it to her mom.

"Your mom must take it for now, but if you're good, I'd hope she'd give you some," he said, and that got a squeal from the youngster.

"Fresh, Mom—it's okay to eat—I've tested some myself," he said, and that got him a nod from her and smiles all around the group.

"I'd like to see what you have here," he said, as more of the people in the area came over to join him. He waved his squad that was strung out behind him to come forward and shoulder their arms too. Soon, there was a large mass of Walkerville citizens milling around the marines. All was nice, Solomon thought as he drifted away to walk the displays of food items the farmers had brought to sell to the towns people. He introduced himself to them all, shook every single hand he could, smiled, and even bought—with another chocolate bar—a tomato to eat. He chomped down on the fresh bright red fruit and slurped the insides, seeds and all. Salt, he'd have loved some salt, but the taste of that stored-up sunshine in the tomato just picked this morning was wonderful.

Never thought a simple fruit like a tomato would taste so good … and so good to see that our just being here is accepted too.

#####

As he daydreamed on the bridge, the Boathi captain was oblivious of what was happening around him.

He was running, with all the strength and ability and skill that he'd had twenty years ago in his youth. He ran and bobbed and weaved among the prey, looking for a bull that he felt would be an adversary that would be worth the effort of the hunt.

Find and then kill prey.

He ran. And ran with other Boathi too, but he was faster and quicker, and he was after the biggest bull he could find—and there it was, over to his left. He slowed to go around a female that was slow in the herd and then sped up to his top gait to see if he could close with the big bull.

Faster. His feet clawed into the turf as he was up on the balls of his feet, his claws gripping the grass as he lengthened his stride and sped up his pace.

Faster. His arms pumped, and they churned as he pushed off a slower young male in his way and continued to gain on the bull.

Faster. His lungs were pumping as much air in and out as possible, and he leaned forward and stretched out his right arm, claws outstretched toward the bull.

He leaned far to his right, as his claws reached to the bull's neck, and with one huge leap, he mounted the bull's back. With both hands, he clawed the bull's neck while throwing an arm over the bull's eyes to blind it.

Not being able to see made the animal slow down as it attempted to stop and yet still throw him off its back.

He grinned to himself and held on firmly as the bull's front legs stiffened as it jammed them into the turf to try to stop, and he swiped with all his might at the jugular vein in the bull's neck. It opened and as the prey's blood flowed from the now open vein and its gait stuttered and then it stumbled, he slid off its side to watch it die.

He smiled. The hunt was a success for him, yet once again, and as he squirmed in his chair, he was suddenly reminded that he was on the bridge of the

Sophon, more than a thousand light years from home and not in the hunt.

The sub-alternate at the helm looked at him as if he was waiting for an answer. But he'd missed the question, so he looked back and said, "What, Sub-alternate, do you mean?"

A Boathi couldn't pale, and the green color of their scales showed no changes at all with any kind of emotion. Yet, the sub-alternate at the helm looked like he was somewhat nonplussed.

"Captain, sorry … I was just asking if you'd as yet read the report that I turned in at the end of the week. And about the scan findings, Captain?" he asked.

He was obviously referring to something that was in the report, the captain knew immediately, but he hadn't read the report. He didn't think that anything would be found as he was hoping he'd be able to do the hunt he'd just fantasized in person in ten days or so. "Why don't you summarize the findings, Sub-alternate?" he asked nicely.

"Captain, just three nights ago, our scans reported that they found a cloud—a small cloud—of beryllium oxide. I dropped the *Sophon* down to two miles, did a full scan, and there were no beryl deposits on the planet itself located there. So the report indicated that. It's the only odd thing that we've found on the planet, so far, Captain," he said.

The captain looked at the sub-alternate and then shook his head. "Sub-alternate, please go to the database and look up beryllium oxide, and put it up on the view-screen, please," he said as he realized this might be important but not in finding a human ship.

The view-screen pulsed, and then there was data on the oxide shown, and it was a long scrollable document that he had no intention of reading.

"Fine, now cross-reference that data with our own nuclear reactor hardware, and please have the keywords plates and foils highlighted for us to see," the captain said.

Again, the Boathi sphere ship computer worked, and in a split windowpane, some of those keywords were highlighted on both sides.

He read. He read again and thanked his lucky stars that he'd remembered that small bit of info from his own education those long years ago in the Nuclear Reactor Basics course.

He almost smiled but squashed that before it hit his face, not that a Boathi really knew how to smile, but they did bare their teeth in that kind of circumstances.

"Sub-alternate, thank you. I know that this is not a generally used comment that you'd ever hear from a captain, but I think that you've stumbled onto something. And the fact that it bothered you enough to present it to me in person today instead of just burying it in a report also speaks well for you. I will notify Boathi HQ about your skill on this, Sub-alternate," he said.

As he looked up at the view-screen, he spoke to the whole bridge crew who were looking at same. "Please note on the left-hand pane the specs where it lists the hardware items that we Boathi make using beryl. Note for me the listing down on line … line forty-three under the reactor area? Note it says plates for the pushing of neutrons in the reflector area of a Boathi nuclear reactor," he said.

"And on the left-hand pane, the notes around a third down, where it talks about those very plates being made of beryl—and what can happen should they begin to break down. Note what it says then at the bottom of that paragraph—under the cautions area? Sub-alternate, can you read that for us, please?"

The sub-alternate read the final sentence in that caution area. "It should be noted that while this oxide is harmful should it be inhaled, BeO has specific nuclear properties, which make it attractive for nuclear applications; low neutron capture cross section and high neutron moderating ability, and if found as an oxide, that means that the reactor plates-slash-foils are under some kind of stress, so check carefully for any H-two-O interference."

Ahh... As he'd remembered, *BeO could be caused by the leakage of water into the beryllium plates-slash-foil structures—something that was a concern but not now.*

Today, what had just happened was that the *Sophon* had found that somewhere down there— upwind of where the cloud had been scanned—lay a Boathi reactor—the missing ship, he assumed.

One had been on Ceti4 more than a decade ago. It had disappeared after reporting with the planetary audit that showed that Ceti4 was not a planet that the Boathi should colonize—so it went on the bombing list instead. But sometime between filing that audit and a full two years later, the ship had disappeared. Called the *Barbuda*, it had disappeared completely. No survival beacons had ever been detected; no survivors; no crash site on Ceti4 nor on its previously visited planets either, should they have gone back to one of them. Not a single detectable item of the *Barbuda* had ever been found.

"*Until today,*" the captain said to himself.

He knew what needed to be done.

He would have to contact Boathi HQ on Boathi Prime to let them know what they'd found.

He would have to show them what the Sophon had found, and the hunt next year would be his.

#####

Black Mage Gelert was not upset—at least on the outside. His face was a mask, and he knew that a part of being the one in the room who had the full power of position over others was his right.

At least that's what he'd always told himself, and today was no different.

He sat on the stool, up close to the table, and looked down at his tablet and again did not frown or load his conversation with any kind of value statements. He simply stated the truth.

"Two years, Banshee Gage, is the time that, so far, you have spent on this aspect of the technology —do I have that correct?"

Facing him, but standing, of course, as banshees were always to stand in the presence of those above them in Castle Magic society, the man flinched somewhat as the time line was mentioned right upfront. A mid-aged man, almost six feet in height, his blond hair cropped short around his head, Gage was the head scientist on-board the *Barbuda*, the crashed Boathi ship buried in the strip mine wall. His job—in fact, his whole career within the society —was based on one thing and one thing only. Find new technology on the ship and make it their own.

He nodded to Gelert but held out his hands, palms up as if he was supplicating to his mage. "Mage Gelert, I am so sorry that the needed technology is so far beyond us … but a gentle reminder, please. That we do not even know what this device does — let alone how to control it and how to bend it's use to our own needs," he said as he glanced at the tabletop in front of them.

On the table lay a small device — a cube of about eight or nine inches on each side. One side held what must be the control panel with a display screen that had some Boathi icons and writing at the top of the control dashboard. That much had been seen as factual and truthful so far. But in the two years since the device had been taken from what was believed to be the Boathi armory — a locked room within the ship that sidearms and some kind of energy weapons had been discovered — nothing more had been found.

"Well," Banshee Gage went on, "we did find out how to charge the device. We did find out how to turn it on, so to speak, by using the Boathi computer in the armory — but what the device does is still unknown in reality. We know that it is a weapon. It has no combustible or flammable contents within same — just normal computer motherboards and a small sub-device that can produce and then mist out a gas. After testing all of the factors that we do know, we still do not know what it is nor for that matter what the gas that is dispelled is supposed to do." He reached forward, picked the cube up, and turned it over in his hands.

Mage Gelert could tell the man was truly stumped, which was not a good thing as he was just about the best and brightest scientist in the castle. If he was stumped ... then we all are, Gelert thought.

He took the liberty of smiling back at Gage. "So, I've read your reports. Seems that no matter what you think you're programming the device to spit out gas-wise, there appears to be no changes to the test subjects—is that still correct?"

That got a big nod from Gage who went on this tangent with passion. "Mage—exactly! We set it for a whole range of what appear to be the various features, then lock it into a sealed room with our test animals, have the device spit out the gas ... and nothing happens. We have tested all the various features—over and over—and are now working on combinations of same-still trying to see what kind of ordnance this device is or what it can do. And so far, not a thing," he said and shook his head negatively.

Mage Gelert held up his hand to stop further discussion right there. "Not a single item seemed to have any effect on the test animals—what were you using anyways?" he inquired.

Gage checked his tablet for a few seconds and then replied. "We are now using a class of rodents —we call them cosmis—as their lifespan is only one year. If anything, that should give us more than enough time to see what effect the gas would have as well as some longer-term span to see how it might take a while for it to impact the cosmi too."

Gelert nodded. He knew testing sometimes meant that an effect of a weapon could often be delayed by design to affect the targets after the fact. He tilted his head. "You said 'now' Gage—what were you using before these cosmi rodents?"

The banshee quickly tapped on his tablet screen and then held it up for his mage to see. On the screen was a small ape-like creature that was about thirty pounds in size according to the citation below the picture.

"We were using this breed of apes—lemmis they're called. Lifespan runs about six years and size about as shown. But there was a problem with our supplier—somehow the purity of the species strain was compromised, and we had to switch off to the cosmi species," he said.

"Compromised? How so?" Mage Gelert asked.

"After having a new group added to our sample troop, they seemed to fit in well with the current stock—all undergoing testing as per normal for almost three months. We kept them in a large, single environment holding area.

"Then, when some of the females gave birth, their young showed some disturbing mutant characteristics that we could not fathom nor quell—

so we ended our use of same," he said as once again his fingers danced on his tablet, and he turned it to show his mage once more.

In the full-screen photo, a close-up of a mother lemmi, cuddling her newborn baby, showed that the infant in fact had two heads—one where it should be and one jutting up and out of its left shoulder. While the normal one was full size for the size of the baby, the shoulder head, Gelert could tell, was very small, yet both had full eyes, noses, and mouths open as they cried.

"Mothers couldn't bear the changes, and all were killed by their mothers within days of birth. So we sanitized the whole testing lab—killed and disposed of all those lemmis, completely cleaned up the whole area—new cages and the like. And we've blacklisted the supplier of those lemmis so that we never run into that again, Mage," he said and dipped his head to show respect.

The mage nodded. *Quite right. Nothing worse than a supposed pure species having changes that came from sloppy breeding at the supplier level.*

"Banshee Gage. Continue. I know that this device is just one of the hundreds we've identified on board this ship that we have no idea what it is or what it does. Continue to delve into that for us, and if you have any special needs, contact me STAT," he said.

200

He rose off his stool and then stopped. "Banshee, would you have any idea as to why there was what looked like some kind of a leak of water all over the deck floors when we came in at the rear? Had to walk halfway here with that sloshing, and it should be looked into too—I know that this is not your own area of expertise, but can I ask, please, that you let the support staff know and have it cleaned up and looked into causally please as well?"

He smiled for the first time at Gage and then left the meeting room on the Boathi sphere ship, the *Barbuda*, to take the long walk back to the spot they'd first gained entry to the ship those many years ago. They'd simply cut a hole into the side of the sphere and then over the years had made a real entry point much bigger and easier to use back near the engines and the Boathi reactor that still powered the ship.

He wished he'd had real boots for a second and then again smiled at himself. *Folks at the top of the heap seldom had the time to worry about this kind of small triviality …*

CHAPTER EIGHT

As Nora looked out the window, up here on the second floor of the arena, the sun was behind a cloud, yet the core of Walkerville looked bright and full of promise as it lay in the distance. With more than forty smart zombies up on the third floor, where the arena offices were, she felt good about their position and the fact they'd been able to hide themselves so well. She wished she had more — more smart zombies with more rifles and even some training. Using a hunting rifle against trained marines with semi-automatics was generally a recipe for disaster.

"*But,*" she said to herself, "*she had the element of surprise.*" She had real intel on the base from some of those who'd been there and worked on the base too.

She had one more thing too that the marines didn't know about either. She had backup and support from three tribes that were on their way here now, from the lands between Walkerville and Maxwell. The three tribes were sending more than a hundred of their tribesmen—well-seasoned hunters—and that made her feel even better as the clouds above moved and sunshine poured down on the town only a mile or so away.

She looked over at the man who sat across from her at the table. "Fred," she said, "let's go over this one more time, shall we?" She pointed at the layout map of the army base. The old map still showed the basic setting of the base with the buildings and the streets that bordered the base too.

Fred rose and walked over to the map on the easel. "We know—we've been in this exact sewer pipe itself as a reminder—that somehow during the attack of last year, it became lodged with one end in the ground. And after some investigation by us just two weeks ago, we saw that the end under the ground had been jammed into a culvert that had been there for years. What that did was to allow raccoons and other scavengers easy access to the base without the worry of digging under or climbing over the frost-wire fence. We knew about it, and it was on our list to fix—then the marines attacked. So we never got to it. But, as I said before," he said as he pointed at the map at the top side where the street lay, "the culvert comes out right about here. It's standard twenty-four-inch culvert pipe, and I figure it's a crawl of about forty yards from the ditch to the inside of the pipe in the base. About, say, a five-minute crawl is what I figure, Nora," he said.

She nodded at him. "Fine, thanks Fred. Your help on this and the general intel on the marine force itself is most appreciated," she said as a man came into the room with a message.

"Nora, the tribes—all three of them, it appears— have just shown up, and they're all downstairs, looking for you, I think?"

She grinned at the man and said, "Let's go see what we got, soldier-wise." She led the way out of the small conference room and down the stairs just to the left. At the bottom, there were a few lights on as the huge windows of the arena had all been boarded up long ago after the Boathi bombing. She turned to her right and went through the glass doorways down the long aisle that had one of the arena ice rinks on one side and the dressing rooms on the other. As she and Fred reached the end of that rink, they went through the double glass doors once more and then through another set and were suddenly among tons of tribesmen.

And what tribesmen they were—rather, as she

corrected herself, *what tribesmen and tribeswomen they were.*

One group stood over on one side of the rink on the cold concrete floor. At the head of that group stood a woman, quiver and bow over her shoulders, with one arm was busy holding a snarling Taxa on a short leash. She stood in front of more than thirty other tribe members. All women. All dressed in leather shorts and some kind of a cross-vest over a long-sleeved jumper top that was brown—sort of a shiny brown like polished chocolate. She knew already that this was the Interstate Tribe—their own given name—but she could see that it sort of fit for them.

To their left stood a man also in front of quite a few others in his tribe. He had, as they all did behind him, a topknot of long hair that was braided and hung down to the middle of their chest. Each was naked to the waist, and most that she could see had tattoos of animals and stripes and the like. Most of the tattoos were in red, and Nora called them the Red Tribe in her own mind. There were also some women, again, dressed like the males, bald except for that topknot, naked to the waist, and just as heavily tattooed too. All of the Red Tribe members had rifles or shotguns though a couple had bows.

Beside them was another group of more than

sixty or seventy tribesmen with three leaders standing in front. This tribe had no name, but she called them the Slaver Tribe as she knew they were very much into attacking villages and taking prisoners to sell in Lindos as slaves. She did think that such efforts were not in the best of ethics, but then she wasn't in their shoes. They were supposed to be pretty fierce fighters though, so that was on her side.

She looked at the leaders one by one and then waved them to approach her. She took the opportunity to introduce herself and to spend some time with each of them, doing what she remembered was called bonding.

Hours later, after all had been fed, the plans for the attack to take back the Walkerville Army Base had been deployed, and all had agreed on their various duties and missions, she was alone once again.

She thought on the mission and about what kind of casualties they would encounter, and she had a sleepless night on the night before their attack.

"Please, enjoy! Fill up on some of our best local fare, and please, I know you have questions, so ask! At Castle Magic, we hide nothing—as you will learn," the warlock said as he sat down at his place, and the rest of the large dinner party did likewise.

In the large ballroom of the castle, tables had been arranged in a large U shape. The warlock and some of his mages sat at the middle table, and beside the warlock, in what Javor thought was the seat of honor, sat Jennifer—their quarry. She was truly identical to their Jessica yet somehow looked different. Smiling delightfully to one and all, she ate delicately and was dressed in a gown that appeared to be covered in some kind of sparkles. *She was the quarry all right,* and Javor knew *it would be a real task to get her out of the castle—but they did have a plan at least.*

Sue and her group were seated at the other two tables, split about evenly between both. And between each of the visitors sat a banshee so that each of the visitors could talk to a castle dweller close at hand.

Sue had asked that each of her group dress for a state dinner, and most of them scratched their heads as not one of them had anything dressy. But each had put on a clean new set of camouflage clothes, and in Vera's case, she actually wore a bright red shift that captured most of the looks of the men. ` Sue, not to be outdone, had a new camouflage outfit that she had added a colored vest to, and she had also fixed her hair.

Javor grinned down into what he was told was

his dinner appetizer and wondered if it was snails. He hoped not but then again, covered in what was some kind of spice and butter and garlic and parmesan cheese too, it could make anything taste good. He took another bite and then a slurp of the castle's favorite beverage—beer of some kind—and leaned back.

"Is it to your liking, Javor?" a voice beside him asked.

He smiled at the banshee woman to his right. "Yes, it truly is great! I should ask if I can get the recipe for the topping … it's so good I think an old army boot would taste good with this on it," he said, and that got a polite smile and titter from her and a few more around them.

Talk went on as the food and beer was consumed. *Some did have wine,* Javor noted, and things got more social. *Alcohol is one of the social lubricants that works,* Javor thought, and he checked that box off for this planet in his mental archive.

As the one called the black mage rose to welcome the visitors and to ask on behalf of Castle Magic why they'd come all this way, the room quieted a bit.

Ahh … down to business, Javor thought, and he turned slightly to his right to look at the warlock during the talks that were to follow.

Sue rose and began to make the presentation to

them. She shared that the Regime was growing and becoming the one real government of Ceti4. As the Regime was in the process of looking for full partners in this re-growth, it was her job to ask on behalf of the Regime for Castle Magic to come on board as a full city-state. They would control their own areas and people and all that entailed but do it under the aegis of the Regime. At this point, it was a small role, and she admitted that, but it would grow. Ambassadors from Castle Magic would be granted full seats at the table—voting seats too—in all decisions to be made by the Regime.

As she talked, Javor studied the warlock. His face betrayed not a single emotion or any kind of opinion about what was being said. However, the warlock fiddled with the end of a fork at the side of his plate. He pushed it one way, then back, and then back again, over and over. When Sue reached to the part about seats at the table, the warlock's fiddling stopped and his hand froze. Javor had no idea what that might mean, But it appeared the comment about seats at the table had affected him to some degree.

The sorceress jumped into the conversation and thanked Sue for the presentation, most likely interrupting the black mage who still stood at the head table. "We thank Sue and our visitors for their visit as well as their presentation. We will take it under consideration and have an answer for the Regime as soon as possible—in less than a few days, I would guess," she said which got a nod from the warlock.

As she spoke, he noticed *some of the banshees nodding in agreement, so at least Sue's offer was received … perhaps as good as it could have been.*

Sue tilted her head. "We will await your counsel and then work out any more details if needs be. In the meantime, could we perhaps offer an aerial tour of your kingdom? For any of you who'd like to take a ride in our floater, we would take you all up and around the areas, from the mountains to the east all across the rolling hills and mesas and hillocks running off to one side. It's pretty impressive and a trip that should not be missed at all …"

That got some real smiles, and the black mage looked at many here at the dinner and nodded to them all, holding up a hand to stop the cries of "Oh, yes … pick me" and the like. He grinned at Sue. "We would love that, and I can promise a large contingent for sure," he said.

Sue nodded and added, "The viewing room seats only twenty—so if we can, say, break your groups into groups of ten each, they'd all see the same tour, and we'd love the smaller groups so we can point out much. The warlock and yourself and the sorceress too are invited as well, of course," Sue said, and Javor held his breath waiting for the answer.

This was it.

The black mage looked at the warlock and saw what he needed to see. "Due to your presentation, we—the warlock and I—will not be able to go this time around, so the sorceress will represent us instead, if that would be acceptable?"

The sorceress squealed and clapped her hands together, and Javor almost grinned as the girl was so, so young.

"Tomorrow then, let's get together at breakfast and work out the groups," Sue said, and that got smiles all around.

CHAPTER NINE

Inside the sewer pipe, Fred crouched behind two of the tribal leaders with their Taxas. They had been sent down the culvert first to chase out any other kind of scavenger they found, and judging by the snarling they heard reverberating in the culvert pipe, it was clear for the rest of the zombie and tribes to enter.

It had taken a bit, Fred knew, for the whole bunch of them—more than 140 or so—to get down the culvert, and they were backed up quite a bit. Ahead of them, the eastern sky was hinting at becoming pink in color, and their assault would start at true first light.

Fred had counseled Nora that the marines had used night goggles before, so they were aware they had to stay to the deepest shadows when they came over the woods and fields across the street from the base. Three times, a Jeep had gone by on the street doing a patrol outside of the base grounds on the streets at those borders. There were twenty minutes between the first and second and then the third one too—so they quickly got their whole group of attackers into the culvert and underground.

Fred nodded to Nora who was beside him in the huge mouth of the sewer pipe. "Nothing has changed here—at least down here at this end of the base, Nora. We should be good to slowly infiltrate up the base main road—off to the side, I'd think—to the barracks. You've already split us up into squads, so each should take their spots outside each of the barracks and await the attack alarm. With surprise on our side—plus the marines are all in bed asleep right now—we should be okay, I'd think," he finished off.

The plan was to have enough forces to allow a squad of ten to enter each of the barracks buildings and shoot every single marine they found—no prisoners. No eating either, Nora had drummed into the few bitten zombies they had among the attack group, and no slave hostages either she'd barked at the tribes. This was payback, and taking over the base was the real mission.

As they crouched, the Jeep made its scheduled pass behind them, the two marines inside talking about some kind of an upcoming party or some such drivel, Fred thought.

Nora gave the good to go to the two tribal leaders in front of her, and Fred followed quickly, moving with some speed across the drill field parallel to the main base road. The dozen barracks buildings were just ahead, all dark and asleep, and he took up a position just off the two wooden steps that led up to the barracks door.

From within, he could hear snoring, as the door had a screen in the top half and it was open to allow in the cooler nighttime air. More than one snore, he could tell, and soon to be none at all.

He checked his rifle—a .303 with a seven-shot clip. He knew there was a shell in the chamber already, and he clicked off his safety, which was louder than he had imagined, and nodded to the other four attackers with him. Shelagh grinned at him and made motions to him to do well with a thumbs-up. At the other end of the barracks, five more attackers were also set to pour into the building, shooting as they came.

It took almost six minutes for everyone to get into position, and when the first shot fired by Nora rung out, they all jumped with excitement as they kicked through the barracks doors, rifles blazing…

#####

"Are you sure, Sub-alternate," the captain asked for the second time.

The helmsman worked again on his console. The sidebar information on the view-screen changed once more and then the icon that meant computing … please wait appeared. After a full minute, the same conclusions were displayed—in bright pink too, all on the *Sophon* bridge noted.

The results read: Confirmed. *Barbuda* ship located at these coordinates. Reactor in safe limits but needs updates. All ordnance in non-armed state except for two gene splicers—one has been used successfully in what appears to have been rudimentary testing."

That did have the captain stumped, but it was of no real issue. Gene splicers worked on a species to change their genes in the next generation by adding a mutation to the species. You could, he knew from an example that he remembered from years ago in his academy classes, use it to make all the females give birth to legless young—effectively winning any kind of war before even declaring same. Why the gene splicer broadcasters had been used was beyond him, but it mattered not a whit.

The *Sophon* had found the *Barbuda*!

Prizes, he thought, *would be in order for the captain of the Sophon.* He wondered what they might be and if he could wrangle a new posting on Boathi Prime itself at HQ even so he could hunt each year.

He showed his teeth and said, "Sub-alternate, compute a course to go and sit right above the *Barbuda*, STAT."

The sub-alternate turned and looked at his captain. "Captain, of course, yes, but I wanted to just gently remind you that the ship lies half-buried in what looks like a strip mine of some kind, only two miles from a heavy concentration of humans in a town nearby. If we do that—just drop down—we could face some kind of aggressive action on their part. Might I make a small suggestion that instead we take a shuttle down to the mine with a small force—all shielded, of course, and investigate with that much smaller Boathi footprint?" he asked.

The captain was surprised at what a great idea that was, but, of course, he could not acknowledge it. "Sub-alternate, yes, that is exactly what I meant when I said 'sit right above.' Do you not understand Boathi tactics?" he intoned, and his face was tight, his scales stretched so tight they were almost humming.

The sub-alternate turned around so quickly that his swivel chair squawked, and his fingers flew over his console keyboard. He worked for a whole minute, double-checked his work, and then half-turned back to his captain.

"My apologies—may your eggs hatch quickly,

CastleMagic

Captain—and I've just sent down that shuttle with a squad for security as well on full shields. They will first find, then enter the *Barbuda*, and once they have it under their control, we will hear back. I have also instituted a live feed—on screen, Captain?" he asked, his voice trying to please.

The captain gave his permission, and the view-screen went blank for a second to be replaced by what was the smaller view-screen of that shuttle craft as it lay in one of the landing ports on the *Sophon*. Moments later, it lifted off, sped out into the planet's atmosphere, and took a hard turn to port. After several minutes of flight down toward the surface close to the mountains that lay below, the shuttle leveled off and sped to the west. It took a minute more, but suddenly, below the shuttle, they could see the strip mine. Its sides were almost a mile apart as the mine had been worked hard over what looked like generations. There were a couple of skids of some ore left on the slanting roadway that curled down the outside edge of the pit—obviously, no mining was going on now. On one side, as the shuttle vectored to starboard, there was a large hole about the size, the captain thought, of a Boathi sphere ship. As the shuttle reached the edge of that hole, dust swelled up in huge clouds as the shuttle braked and then settled on the roadway halfway up from the bottom of the pit.

Moments later, the view changed from the shuttle to a cam carried on someone's shoulder as the view was one of someone running toward that hole that lay in front of the shuttle. There were more than ten of these sub-alternates, and the captain was able to identify that most, at least as far as he could see, were wearing the shield belts.

As they entered the hole, there was no hindrance from any human. They got to the back of the *Barbuda* and went up a set of wooden stairs to a hole that had been carved into the side of the ship.

"Not one of our own entry points," the sub-alternate on the bridge said.

"Obviously," the captain replied as the first of the shuttle squad entered the ship.

The squad went down a set of stairs to a deck the captain thought was in engineering, near the rear of the ship. The wearer of the cam slogged through some water on the deck heading forward toward the bridge area. As they walked, they made some noise as the water on the deck sloshed around, and when they rounded a corner, a human stood there.

"Wait … what the hell," the human man said and pointed at them. "Boathi. You are Boathi and our enemy," he said as he began to back up quickly.

One of the shuttle squad up front used a wand on him, and he fell back on the deck, his head glancing off a bulkhead as he went down. The Boathi wearing the camera stopped to look down at the human, and the sidebar lit up with his voice recording. "Human, male, about thirty-five years, six feet, approximately one hundred and eighty pounds, brown hair, blue eyes. Wearing what looks like a white coat of some kind over human shirt and slacks. Some kind of a technician, I'd postulate," the Boathi squad leader said, and then he moved on.

At a juncture of three main corridors in the sphere ship, they split up. Half headed for the bridge of the *Barbuda*, and the other half headed for crew quarters to investigate the whereabouts of the *Barbuda* crew.

As the crew quarters group turned to port and then crossed a major corridor, there was a shout from down that side aisle.

"Boathi … there's Boathi on board," some human yelled out and would have gone on until a wand silenced him.

As they advanced down a side corridor now, trying to stay off the main corridors of the ship, they turned another corner and were met with four humans who blocked their way. Each was wearing some kind of a black robe, open down the side, with those human slacks and shirts underneath.

The Boathi leader said, "Kill them," and at the front of the group, three Boathi with wands sprayed the humans.

The humans did not fall. They sprayed the Boathi back with the same wands—to no effect.

Each of the humans, the captain could see, wore a belt shield that had been turned on and was protecting them. Each of the humans also bore a wand—and knew how to use them as well. Each side, Boathi and human, was evenly matched, shield and weapons alike.

"Standoff!" The captain roared his displeasure...

At the foot of the main road off to the side of the castle, Zoe lay and awaited their tour visitors. The gravel road went on and into the castle, across the river that acted like a moat and the drawbridge too, but here a few hundred yards away, the floater just waited out of the way. Not the best position tactically, Javor thought, but it'd have to do.

At the bottom of the catwalk, Sue had been resourceful and had put together a waiting area. Those who were there for a ride but not in the actual group could sit and wait in a bit of comfort. She'd raided one of the storage areas, and more than thirty chairs were arranged around a table or two that held cold drinks. Wayne had even rustled up some hors d'oeuvres for them to munch on while the tours went on. They had no idea as to who would be in which tour group nor for that matter how many there were even going to be.

As the gate opened up on the castle, two dozen castle inhabitants walked out, and they did sound excited, Javor thought. Taking a ride on the floater was not a biggie to him, but to others, being up high in flight might be exciting. "Least we hope so," he said to himself.

As the group came closer, he could see the sorceress, Jennifer, was accompanied by two of her banshees.

No mages, he hoped. Mages were invulnerable, and they supposedly had magic wands that could kill.

He'd never seen the wands, but the magic spell that kept Bruce's bullet from killing that gray mage as they'd been greeted just yesterday was impressive.

Would love to have one of those myownself, he thought. He smiled as the group presented itself in the bright sunshine on this clear summer day.

The banshee who must have been the head banshee looking after the sorceress spoke up first. "We would like to thank you, Sue and all of you, for the chance to see our kingdom from your floater. It will be a really enjoyable experience," he said, as he gestured to the sorceress beside him. "We would like the sorceress to be in the first group of ten that you've requested for us to take the ride and she is—as you can see—very excited to do just that," he said dryly.

Jennifer smiled shyly, but she nodded her head vigorously and skipped forward for a few steps.

"Might we ask—if this is allowed—" Sue said, "to get, say, the sorceress and her banshees to take up a position on the gangplank so that we could take a photo or two to present to the warlock later today?"

It all came down to this. No mage meant there was no real danger to the group. Banshees could be injured, and that was what the group counted on.

At his waist, a sudden vibration on his monitor warned him of an incoming notification—but he had to postpone that look as what was happening in front of him took precedence.

As the head banshee nodded, Javor thought, *Bingo*, and took up his position at the end of the gangplank. He had a big camera on his belt, and he raised it up and began to give the posing instructions to one and all. "We'd like Sue and the sorceress at the front of the photo with her banshees and our group behind them, if that's okay?" he asked. "The rest of the first group, just wait here for the photos to be taken and then come on up and into the floater behind us," he said.

Wayne and Jon pushed up the gangplank about ten feet and then turned to face downward. The two banshees came next and slid up the gangplank to stand right in front of Wayne and Jon. Perfectly positioned to be captured, Javor thought, as he played with the lens of the camera, sighting it, and adjusting the dials and settings.

"Lastly, our honored duo," he said, as Sue took the sorceress's arm and led her up to stand in front of the banshees.

All were in position, and Javor took his place in front of the gangplank, a few feet off the prow of same.

Someone behind him shouted, "Boathi ... that's a Boathi shuttle ship," and all hell broke loose.

Javor quickly gave a thumbs-up, and above him, Toby saw same, and Zoe went up in a rush as their plan went into action.

Javor jumped quickly for the rapidly rising gangplank and saw that both Wayne and Jon had the jump on the two banshees in front of them. They had quickly put them in chokeholds and had swung them off their feet and over the side to the ground as it fell away.

Two down, the sorceress in their hands ... but Boathi, Javor thought, they've found me...

#####

Thanks SO much for the read!

If you've the time too, to write a review on this dystopian adventure, I'd love to have you go to Amazon and post same....

We writers work in a solitary environment so your comments and reviews are read and studied....and at least in my case, I try to learn from same.

Much obliged...and wait for the next BONE Series book entitled Patch Bridge!

Jim Rudnick